*Veiled Secrets*
*Glass House Books*

**Josie Montano** is an international award-winning author with 25 years of experience in the industry. With nearly 70 books published, she champions advocacy and celebrates diversity. A dedicated storyteller since the age of 9 (when she wrote her first book for the school library), her work inspires and empowers readers worldwide.
Website: booksbyjosie.com.au
Facebook: JosieMontanoAuthor
Twitter: @JosieMontano
Instagram: josiemontano1

**Archie Fusillo** grew up in Melbourne, Australia, the son of Italian immigrants. Surrounded by wonderful storytellers, he learned early the value of stories shaping our lives and connecting people, irrespective of backgrounds and is now an award-winning author sharing his multitude of stories, books, and articles about growing up as a first-generation Italo-Australian.
Website: archimedefusillo.com
Twitter: @ArchieFusillo

The Collaboration
Josie and Archie met at a children's literature festival and realized they had more in common than just being of Italian background and writing: their parents come from villages a stone's throw apart! Immediately, ideas, stories, characters, and laughter came pouring out. Veiled Secrets incorporates their own history, culture, traditions, and family values.

**Glass House Books**
an imprint of IP (Interactive Publications Pty Ltd)
Treetop Studio • 9 Kuhler Court
Carindale, Queensland, Australia 4152
sales@ipoz.biz
http://ipoz.biz/shop

Printed in 12 pt Adobe Caslon Pro on 14 pt Avenir Book

ISBN: 978192830913 (PB); 978192830920 (eBk)

A catalogue record for this
book is available from the
National Library of Australia

# VEILED SECRETS

## Archimede Fusillo
## &
## Josie Montano

Glass House Books
Brisbane

We dedicate this book to our past, present, and future. In particular, to our parents who migrated here, stamping their Italian footprints into Australian soil, not only to make a better world for themselves and their descendants, but also to introduce their passion, culture, and traditions to this young country. Their sacrifices have been fruitful, and we will always remember them through our enduring stories.

## CHAPTER ONE ~ Nicola

Nonno Nicola refuses to let anyone help with the cooking when he has the family over. Mum fusses and complains. She tells Nonno that he's being a hard nut and a head case, but Nonno doesn't seem to mind. My Zia Angela, Mum's sister, tells Mum to accept the fact that at his age, mid-seventies, Nonno Nicola is old enough to refuse help from his kids if he wants.

Mum tells her sister to get a grip on reality. When the immediate family visits Nonno's for a meal, that meal involves fourteen people, Nonno Nicola included.

"When I come to your house, you cook for me," Nonno says. "When I invite you to my home, you eat what I give you and you don't complain."

"Listen to your dad and stop complaining, Martina," Zia Angela grins.

But it's not that Mum's complaining. It's just that since Nonna Rocchina died, Nonno Nicola has been refusing outside help and the house is looking a bit shabby.

Not falling apart shabby, just not clean-as-a-whistle shabby. The kind of shabby that in less obsessive families is actually a kind of welcoming lived-in kind of relaxed shabby.

The garden is mickey-smick though. There isn't a leaf out of place. There isn't a weed daring enough to poke its spindly head out in Nonno's little patch of the world. Not unless they want to get blasted with a shot of my grandfather's homemade pesticide.

I grin at Nonno and grab the last few slices of his homemade salami before my cousin Ricky spies them.

"Now, you *mangia*. Eat." Nonno smiles at me. "I got plenty more salami I can cut up."

1

Just then, Zia Angela reaches across the table and snatches some of the precious salami from my plate.

"Poor Ricky always misses out," she says, slapping the slices on a tearaway length of bread and handing it to my younger cousin.

Like he really needs more salami to make him look even more like the before shot in some never-fail diet scam.

I'm about to grab the salami back when I get an eyeful from Mum from across the patio. She's simultaneously heaping potato salad into Dad's plate, directing my sister Danny towards the lamb on the spit Nonno Nicola has got rigged up, and giving me that look that turns blood to jelly.

"Try not to eat the plate if you can help it, Rick," I say instead, because I know it will get the little fiend all fired up. He hates being reminded that for a thirteen-year-old he's about the size a Japanese-built people mover. My Zia Angela hates it even more.

"He's big boned," she snaps. "It's not nice that you say those things, Nick."

I wipe the grin from my face but not from my eyes and give Ricky a slow wink. I'm about to go help myself to some mushroom risotto when Nonno Nicola calls for everyone's attention.

Nonno Nicola is retired now. Has been for about five years. He was working as a painter with the railways at the time. Before that, he worked as a cobbler, the trade he brought with him from Italy back in the late 1960s when he was just eighteen.

I'm named after Nonno Nicola. My baptism name is Nicola Angus Donaldson. Everyone calls me Nick. Everyone save for Nonno Nicola. He calls me Nicola. He says it's a name with distinction because for generations the first-born son on his side of the family has been named Nicola. I've got a zillion cousins and uncles in Italy whose name is Nicola apparently. The Angus part is due to my mum insisting that since Dad's side of the family don't have the tradition of naming rights, it would be nice if I had my other grandfather's name as a middle name.

"I need everyone to listen to me carefully," Nonno Nicola starts. He's standing by the lamb spit, sort of barring it from the hungry masses with his skinny frame.

Danny is caught with a slice of lamb hanging off the side of her plate. She looks startled, not sure whether she should stand her ground or make a rush for a seat next to Dad. After a moment's hesitation, she does neither. She leans against the brick pillar that holds up the veranda instead.

I shake my head at her, just to let her know I think she looks like an idiot standing there holding her plate like some pagan offering. Danny pokes her tongue out at me.

"Nicola!" My Nonno's voice slaps me in the face.

"Yes, Nonno?"

I can feel my face blushing. I hate it when he calls me Nicola in that tone of voice that suggests I might be somewhat impaired.

"You finish you game with you sister?" he asks. I nod and give Ricky a glare, daring him to even pretend to snigger at my expense. Ricky glances down into his beans and corn mash.

There are seven of us cousins. Besides Danny and me, there's the Japanese people mover, his younger brother Marco, and his even younger brother Fernando. We call them Mark and Fred. Only Ricky—real name Riccardo—has a nickname. It cuts him up really bad. His brothers think it's funny. Then there's Monica and Samuel. They belong to my Uncle Nick, Nonno's baby—he was a surprise birth I'm told. Mum and Zia Angela were in secondary school when he was born. Yeah, they were surprised!

"I hope you have all been enjoying the food," I hear Nonno say. I look up and he's smiling at his daughters and Uncle Nick who's also really Nicola.

"I am very happy to have my family here with me today." Nonno continues in Italian now. "I hope my daughters don't judge my cooking too badly, eh…"

"No, Papa," my mum cuts in. She does a kind of half-grin, half-grimace and looks at her sister as though she ought to have an input.

But Zia Angela doesn't get the drift and says simply, "Since when do we judge food in this family? We cook. We eat." Then she glances around, a thin grin on her face.

"Anyway," Nonno continues, "there is a special reason why I asked everyone to be here today."

Nonno Nicola pauses and that gives Mum time enough to ask if there's something wrong with him, like maybe he's announcing he's contracted some disease, or he's discovered Nicola isn't a family name handed down the generations.

"I'm going to Italy," Nonno Nicola says in a flourish. "One more time, before I die, I want to see my village again. I want to breathe the air of Castel Pulcinella Velato just once more. After so many years, I want to visit my village and be part of the special celebrations they are planning for this year's Festa Della Madonna. It's exactly one hundred and fifty years this year that they found the statue of the Madonna in the grotto outside the village, and I want to be there and be a part of it. For my beautiful Rocchina, too."

My jaw is doing a fair imitation of an unhinged door when Nonno pipes up with even more startling news.

"I have put the names of all my grandchildren in my cap," he says and takes the peaked cap from his head and shows us the pieces of paper secreted there. "I am going to draw out one name, and if my daughters or son, depending on which of my grandchildren's names is drawn, approves, I will take that grandchild with me. At my expense."

For a few minutes, there is a kind of frantic babble of voices, my mum and Zia Angela mostly, but Dad and Uncle Nick too. The kids just sort of look at each other like maybe we've all misheard. Even the Japanese people mover has stopped chewing and is looking confusedly at Nonno Nicola.

"You can't be serious. Going to Italy, with one of the kids, at your age?"

Uncle Nick is never smooth with language. He only ever really opens his mouth to change feet.

But the comment is enough to make Nonno Nicola see red. "What? You people think that I'm weak in the head?" Nonno fumes. "I thought you would be pleased one of the children gets to see where this family is from..."

"Part of this family," Dad corrects.

Nonno ignores Dad and after getting silence again, says calmly. "It is something I have to do. Please, understand." And before anyone can argue or comment, he reaches into his hat and pulls out a folded bit of paper.

I look at Danny. She's standing on the tips of her toes, as though that will be enough to get her name read out.

Mark and Fred are wide-eyed, their necks craned so that their heads look as though they've sprouted from long stalks.

The Japanese people mover has abandoned his food and is seriously staring at Nonno Nicola's closed right fist. There are the beginnings of tears in the corners of his eyes from the strain.

Monica and Samuel are locked in a kind of semi-wrestler hold embrace, like that might lead to Nonno Nicola declaring them dual winners.

"Why not take one of your own kids, the girls, or Nick?" Dad pipes up suddenly. "I bet Martina would love to go." He looks at Mum and I see her give a sheepish grin. Of course, Mum would love to go to Italy, I think. Dad's been promising her he'll take her one day for about ten years now.

"And what about Ange," Uncle Roman offers. "Ang is the eldest. It makes sense that she should go..."

I look at Uncle Nick's wife, Aunty Stella. She rolls her eyes. Uncle Nick has enough to do in Australia trying to get their new house built, I see her think. He ain't going nowhere.

"Nicola."

I hear the name, but it doesn't register for a few seconds.

"Nicola."

Unmistakable this time.

It's odd but there's no sound in my life for about a full minute. It's as though by reading out my name, my Nonno has sucked all other sounds right out of the air.

Only when my sister hits me clean in the middle of the forehead with an empty plastic cup do I hear the commotion that has exploded all around me.

And by then all the others either hate me, envy me, or both.

I just stand there and let Nonno Nicola give me a hug as he whispers in my ear, "It is just."

## CHAPTER TWO ~ Aurelia

"Oh my God, Nonna!" I hug my grandmother.

"*Gu* heppy?" Nonna asks in broken English.

"I love you!"

Nonna sits there with a smug look on her face. She knows what she had just done, she knows she has made my dreams come true, hang on, every teenage girls' dreams come true. Italy! I can't believe it—Italy? The fashion capital of the world. Milan, Rome, Florence—all the cities I've dreamed about, well, since I was old enough to read Mum's fashion mags. The clothes, gold, jewellery, clothes, hot guys, and did I mention clothes?

We'll probably just do a flyby visit to Nonna's home village, the name of it I never remember ' cause it's too long but I'm guessing we'll spend most of our time in the cities. I grabbed my mobile, I couldn't wait to text Sara—she was going to freak out! She was going to be so jealous.

Nonna had invited us all to the winery for lunch that day. It didn't seem like it was going to be any more special than all the other Sunday lunches. We always eat the same thing. Italians love their food, and love the same food all the time, over and over, I'm sick of olives, cheese, salami and pasta already!

Sunday lunch at the vineyard restaurant was a pretty regular thing after Nonno Vito died. The vineyard was built from scratch by my grandfather. I can remember the number of times he'd tell the story of how it all started. "Was joost one hundra dollas dis land." He'd swiftly sweep his arm across like he was back-slapping a lying, cheating real estate agent, 'Now isa one hundra million dollas!' His idea for a winery was laughed at by not only the locals but his own people. "But I spit on dems now!" he would say defiantly and then spit over the balcony onto the ground. Gross!

7

Nonna told me once how she'd met Nonno. Apparently, she came out here when she was only sixteen and lived with some family who were here already. Then she was introduced to Nonno and she knew she was going to marry him. Nothing romantic like it was love at first sight or anything, but she was going to make a good life for herself.

"Aurelia, you must look at da future when you choose da husbands," she advised.

She could see that Nonno had potential and I'm not sure but maybe he'd already started the vineyard—he was a little older than her. She told me that her first boyfriend back in her village was poor and she would have had a hard life, so when that didn't work out, she was determined to find a husband who could look after her.

I asked her if she loved Nonno.

"Not in da beginnings, he was just a husband, but den slowly slowly I love him." She paused and did the sign of the cross. "He was a good man."

I think that sounds a bit shallow. But who am I to judge my Nonna? She's a good person too, so who knows what led her to decide this path? And in those days eighty percent of the marriages were arranged anyhow.

"You want to live da lifes of a farmer wife, or a Signora?" She answered her own question. "I choose da Signora!"

I guess it makes sense, but I'd prefer love more than money. But, if she'd married that farmer, she'd be out picking potatoes on the land or some other kind of vegetable, washing the goats, or even walking the donkey ten kilometres a day, I don't know but I guess it'd be pretty hard, so I don't blame her in a way.

Nonno once told me his side of the story. "She was da most bootiful gals who come out of Italia." He kissed his bunched-up fingers. "She had the big eyes joost like you, and she dress up like a *principessa*, a princess." He sighed, "I knew I was going to marry her straight aways."

My grandmother has just announced at that family lunch that she is taking me with her to Italy. Mum squirms in her seat, and Dad beams proudly I guess he is happy because it's his mum who is taking me. I know why Mum feels uncomfortable: she and Nonna don't really get on. Italian mother and daughter-in-law stuff is worse than the soapie daughters and mothers-in-law. I don't really get it. I mean, I do, 'cause sometimes I see the way Nonna treats Mum, but then a lot of their stuff happened a long time ago, before I was even born.

Mum told me that once Nonna visited when Dad wasn't home and lectured her about looking after her son better and stuff. I mean, the guy was a big boy and married; cut the umbilical cord already. So Nonna has given Mum a hard time over the years, and I know that Mum has always wanted to take me to Italy herself and had been waiting for me to finish school, so Nonna got in first—but, hey, I don't care who takes me, I'm just glad I'm going!

"But, Ma, Lia has…" Mum starts.

"No buts!" Nonna cuts her down without even looking at Mum. "I take Aurelia with me a l'Italia, to show my home country."

Nonna turns away and ignores Mum. Dad is still smiling like one of those clowns at the carnival until he catches sight of Mum glaring at him: it's one of those "Say something to your mother" looks. Like mother, like son. I guess—Dad just turns away and ignores Mum too!

Mum is outnumbered, and unfortunately, I am glad about that. Poor mum. She sits there and sulks and you know when my mum is pissed because she even rejects dessert, and we know she has a sweet tooth.

"Aurelia, my only *nipotina*, my only grandchild," Nonna said. "She deserves to see where I come from, where she come from, eh, Aurelia?" Nonna holds my chin with her thumb and finger and wiggles it from side to side.

I'm named after Nonna. My real name's Aurelia—but apparently that was too hard for my first-grade teacher to say so she started calling me Lia, which I don't mind. I think Mum didn't mind either 'cause she didn't want to call me after her monster-in-law, as Mum calls her, in the first place. So, Lia has stuck, and it's been my name since.

But Nonna hates 'Lia'. She refuses to use it and is the only person who calls me by my birth name.

"I not been back to Italy for sixty years." Nonna looks sad for a split second. "But we gonna have a good time," Nonna smiles, squeezes me and at the same time glares at my mother.

"Nobody going to spoil our trip… nobody."

## CHAPTER THREE ~ Nicola

Mum cried and hugged me for about three hours. Dad shook my hand and patted me on the back. Danny reluctantly gave me an air kiss. Everyone else stood around looking sheepish, especially my luckless cousins. Zia Angela and Uncle Nick kept adjusting the strap to Nonno Nicola's shoulder bag, all the while trying to look as though they were over the disappointment that their kids had missed out on the trip of a lifetime.

Well, I guess it could be the trip of a lifetime, if Nonno doesn't get all old-person sick on me, if we don't lose each other in some foreign airport, if I don't forget to keep an eye on his medication and unwittingly send Nonno Nicola into a diabetes induced coma or worse.

*** 

In the three weeks since Nonno's announcement, everything has been a bit of a blur. Just as well I had my passport from the family trip to Fiji last Christmas. And just as well I'm not exactly sitting at the back of my class academically or there would have been no way Mum and Dad would have let me board this plane.

"You couldn't stretch the pension to First Class, Nonno?" I ask him, grabbing the warm dinner roll off his tray. After all, he has to watch his carb intake. I do it for his own good.

"They give you slippers and champagne in First Class," I tell him. "There's heaps more legroom, too. And you can lie back and sleep like you're in bed."

"When I came to Australia," Nonno begins, and already I'm dreading having opened my mouth about creature comforts. And off he goes. I get the full, unabridged version of how he went to Australia when he was still a young man, how he boarded in a

11

house with four other blokes from his part of Italy, how he rode a beat-up bike to work at the plastics factory...

Thankfully, he falls asleep not long after our brief Brisbane stopover and so does his recollection. I climb over him and decide to take a stroll.

Planes are awesome. Pity they won't let you in the cockpit anymore. At least that might break the boredom. I've got another fifteen or so hours ahead of me yet. Small price to pay, I guess, for missing a few weeks of school, a major Science exam, and the formal. Not that anyone had asked me to partner them or anything. Still.

There are heaps of families on this flight, and a lot of ankle biters. They're swarming over each other making enough noise to drown out the powerful engines I've come to stand by one of the over wing doors to stare at.

It's not like I'm into jet engines or anything, but I like the way the navigation lights play off them, the red and green flickering along the leading edge of the wing and the barrel of the engines. If it wasn't so dark out there, and if we weren't at 40,000 feet or something, I might even take a walk along that wing and check out the scene firsthand.

"You waiting?"

I look around, and it's a girl. She's really close. She's standing almost pressed up against me.

"You waiting?" she asks again.

"I don't think the bus comes this way," I say because it's the first thing that pops into my head. Duh! Real cool.

"Whatever," she huffs and turns away. I look past her and realise my mistake. We're standing outside the toilet. She's asking if I'm waiting to use the toilet.

She's got her back to me now. She's leaning up against the bulkhead and looking towards the pointy end of the plane, the end where the rich people sit. The rich people and the ones who have bosses who pay the big dollars to sit in the plush seats that are like armchairs with built-in TVs, stereo systems, call buttons, fold-out tables, and even recline almost into a horizontal position so you can sleep properly.

"Snobs, I reckon," I say, because I need to erase the bus comment. "They get champagne and peanuts and even menus from which to choose their meals." I nod to myself and check out the girl's profile.

Pretty. Real pretty.

"They have ensuites and stuff up that end of the plane," I continue.

I figure she's worth chatting to. Any conversation has got to be better than listening to Nonno Nicola tell me about his village and how the two of us are going to share some great times during the Festa. As if.

"My name's Nick," I offer, and grin. "And no, I'm not waiting to use the toilet." A sound escapes from my mouth. It's a kind of choked half-laugh, half-yelp. It happens when I think I've just made a poor first impression even worse with a totally useless second attempt.

The girl doesn't answer. She sighs loudly and shuffles on the balls of her feet. She must be keen to get into the toilet.

"There are other toilets down the back of the plane," I tell her helpfully, but not helpfully enough that she wants to thank me or anything.

A moment later and the toilet door opens. A very large woman heaves herself out and tries to push past the girl and me.

"Sorry," she wheezes and smiles thinly. "Could you guys just step into the galley area for half a sec so I can..." She doesn't finish her sentence. Silent-girl and I get her drift and we manoeuvrer into an even tighter space between banks of storage compartments.

It takes the woman a few goes but eventually she manages to get across to her side of the aircraft, and someone manages to beat silent girl into the recently vacated toilet.

"They shouldn't let just anyone fly," she spits and shakes her head.

I'm about to tell her that flying is a democratic right for anyone who can afford the airfare, when quiet girl struts off back toward the pointy end of the plane.

I don't follow her or anything, but I see her flop into one of the aisle seats, one of the posh aisle seats at the end of the plane where the champagne is served in proper fluted glasses, and the luggage gets its own priority sticker.

"You should stay up your end," I whisper in her general direction, and make a mental note to use one of the posh toilets at some stage during the flight, if I can get past the flight attendant who seems to barricade that part of the plane from the rest of us, that is.

Nonno Nicola is snoring loudly when I get back to my seat in the poor section of the plane where they don't give you champagne or little cold cuts of meat and cheese on crispy biscuits. He has his head thrown back and his mouth is open wide enough so that even the pilot can look down into his gullet. Not a pretty sight.

Not like quiet-snobby-girl from up the pointy end. She looks hot, in a standoffish sort of way.

I feel like a major dork. I mean, my comment about the bus was just stupid enough to get me a reputation as a nerd—if it had happened at school with my mates around. Luckily, here on the plane no one heard it. Just the cool girl with the cute dimples and the way-too-smooth skin.

Good one!

"Will he snore like that all the way to Europe?" the guy across the aisle suddenly asks me. He's got a laptop open on the food tray and has his sleeves rolled up as though he's doing some serious stuff right here and now.

Obviously, his boss didn't want to fork out the money for the extra workspace he would have up near Miss Dimples. Either that or this guy's just as hard up for cash as the rest of us, travelling with our knees jammed under our chins.

"I dunno," I answer. "We've never flown to Europe before so my Nonno might just snore part of the way." I give the guy a thin grin and reach over to gently push Nonno Nicola's mouth shut. He shrugs awake the moment my fingers brush up against his chin.

"We there yet?" he asks in Italian. He shifts in his seat and yawns expansively. "Where we is?"

"Somewhere over Australia still," I say.

"Oh."

Just then, we hit a pocket of turbulence. The 'fasten seatbelt' sign flashes on, and I have to help Nonno adjust his belt. He has it so loose about his waist it might as well be down around his ankles.

"Thanks," he whispers. "You is a good boy, Nicola. You see how much you going to like my village."

"Yeah, well, we'll have to wait and see because I don't speak much of the language, and I reckon it might be a little strange for me and them to *capisce* one another."

Nonno Nicola puckers his lips and nods. "Just like was hard for me when I comes Australia. No one he is understand me. But slowly you can make the understand much better."

The plane rocks a bit as Nonno talks. I'm looking out of the window most of the time, at the darkness, and the faint navigation lights reflecting ahead of where we're sitting. I don't see what Nonno Nicola does until he taps me on the back of the head and shoves his cap under my nose. I see that he hasn't taken the bits of paper with all us grandkids names on them out yet.

"You having another lucky draw?" I smile and point at the bits of paper.

Nonno shakes his head, then he winks slowly and touches the side of his nose the way he does when we play cards as a team.

"Take the papers," he instructs me. "Take them."

I shake my head now. Nonno Nicola loves games, so I play along. "And the winner is…" I say with a flourish, pull the first folded note from the cap, and read the name, "Nicola!"

I'm a little surprised at pulling my name from the cap, but I figure Nonno must have dropped the paper back into the cap after the announcement, so I reach for a second. What a coincidence for my name to be pulled out twice in a row.

I open the second slip of paper and read, "Nicola!" And the third. And the fourth.

All seven slips of paper have my name on it.

"It is just," Nonno whispers. "Nicola. My name. Your name. Is just."

Is just what? I want to ask but a violent sideways lurch makes me jump in my seat and I let the moment pass.

## CHAPTER FOUR ~ Aurelia

Mum isn't surprised when the airport staff informs us that I have excess luggage.

"I told you that you packed too much!" she exclaims in front of the check-in staff. Too much? How can I leave behind my three pairs of jeans, all favourites 'cause everything else works around them, my brand-new leather jacket that I got especially for the trip, even though Mum said, "Why bother? Italy is famous for its leather."

Hey, I'll just buy another one!

And how can I survive without my hair straightener, all my makeup, and whatever else there is that's filled my suitcase and makes it look like a plump pillow stuffed with duck feathers?

Thanks to Nonna who just pays the excess, I don't have to make any decisions about what I am going to leave behind or worry about how I am going to pay for excess. Even though we are travelling first class and get more check-in weight for our dollar. I still went over the limit!

"Eh, if she needs, she need!" Nonna glares at Mum. Sometimes the raging war between her and my mother comes in handy for me.

"Yeah," I sneer at Mum. "I need everything!"

"Be smug now, but you've got a lot to face up to when you get home, my dear!" Mum kindly reminds me.

Mum starts to cry as Nonna and I walk away. I know they are tears of sadness; she is going to miss me. But then again, they may be tears of happiness; she is going to be Nonna-free for a month!

The last thing I see before we turn the corner is Dad putting his arm around Mum. I am going to miss them, but I am not going to miss my life. Don't get me wrong, I love my life, but I need a change, a temporary diversion.

"Would you like a champagne?" the steward asks, not realising I am underage.

*First class, ahhh.* I sigh as I take the glass. This is the life, champagne, slippers, reclining seats so you can really sleep! More leg room than economy, and we even choose our meals from a menu.

Nonna flies in style. Apparently, when she migrated to Australia, she came by boat and was sick for the whole month. Thank goodness she can now afford a little luxury. I felt a bit sorry for the people sitting in those seats down the back. Imagine sitting in the same seat for nearly a whole day. It's bad enough when you have to fly two hours domestic; your bum gets numb, and you have elbow fights with the person next to you, about who commands the armrest. And sometimes you have to listen to their boring and pathetic life story and then you have to eat those crappy meals, a little like prison food, not that I know what that's like, but I can just imagine.

Nonna even gave up her window seat for a little while. I lay there looking over the white marshmallow clouds and think of the life I have just left behind. It'll still be there when I get back. It's nice to get away, have a break, but I'll miss Sara, my friends, my mobile and laptop.

About four hours into the flight, I am not only busting to go but want to get away from Nonna's Italian version of *Bold and the Beautiful.* I heard everything about her family, her mother, her brother, her friends, most of them dead, but she is obviously feeling sentimental now that she is heading back to Italy. Then occasionally she'll cry, and I have no idea why! The stories just keep coming out, followed by tears and I just keep nodding my head.

"Nonna, I gotta go."

I head towards the toilets and wonder what the first-class toilets look like. Marble? Self-flushing? It's sad that I can't wait to use them! But there is already a line up.

The stewardess tells me I can use the ones further back. Further back? Does that mean down there? I look back—there is a curtain dividing first class from economy. Ok, so I head down the other end of the plane and pass through the curtain. There is no queue, but the toilets are occupied, so I decide this is better than my first option. Well, there is one guy standing there with his back to me, but I'm not sure if he is checking out the stewardess or waiting for the toilet.

"You waiting?" I ask.

He turns and I get some stupid answer about a bus. Whatever! I am really busting now so am not in the mood for planes, trains and automobile jokes. I look back to see screaming kids, and uncomfortable people shifting about in their seats. I lean against the bulkhead and look towards where I'd come from; quiet, serene, but with that toilet line up already! Maybe all the people in economy have come to our side of the plane to use the toilets. No fair!

The dorky looking guy is trying to chat me up. All I could hear is mumbling, mumbling, I'm not listening. Although I do sort of pick up his name. Rick, I think. Like I care. Oh, and that he doesn't need the toilet, phew!

Finally, the toilet door unlocks. A lady who looks like she's eaten too many burgers in her life squeezes out of the door, and the smell that follows her is enough to make me sick. She can't get past us and asks us to move. I look at the guy and we shuffle to one side, we are pretty close, too close for people who don't know each other. He smells good, better than the toilet anyhow. Once fat lady gets past, this other guy pushes past me to go into the toilet first. Go for it, mate! You may never come out again. I've decided it's not worth it and my bladder just has to hold on a little longer, just enough for us to use the real toilets. So, I walk off and sit back down in my seat. Boy, who knew that going to the toilet was going to be such a drama!

Nonna opens her eyes and smiles. "You go to toilet?" she asks sleepily.

"No, Nonna, it's too busy." I recline my seat.

"You a good gal, Aurelia," she says as she closes her eyes again.

Dream on, Nonna. I don't want to burst her bubble, but, really, I'm not a good girl.

# CHAPTER FIVE ~ Nicola

I'm still reeling from the fact that Nonno Nicola rigged the draw when he lands another newsflash on me. Only now we're about to step off the plane in Rome. It's not enough that for the past fourteen hours I've had to listen to him avoid telling me why he did what he did, except to say, "It is just." Like that explains it all.

There are people everywhere. Not just around you, but all over you. It's wall to wall, ceiling to floor people; most of them like me and Nonno, rushing to get through Customs so they can meet family and friends, or maybe get started on their holiday.

"Some things what you might hear in my village," he says with great care, "maybe you not going to like too much. But don' you worry youself, is not make any difference to me and you have good time."

*Well, that's good,* I'm thinking, because I don't want to worry, but when Nonno takes me by the shoulders the moment the lady in Customs gives us the green light to enter the main terminal, I start to worry.

"Listen, Nicola," he begins in Italian. "Some people in my village have never gone further than the next town in all the years I've been in Australia. They are still simple people. Some have the ways of old still running in their veins. Ignorance is a curse. You understand, Nicola?"

My Nonno's eyes are bloodshot from lack of sleep. I guess he thinks what he's saying makes sense right now, so I nod. "Yeah, I get it. Some people in your village don't like to travel."

Nonno Nicola slaps me on the left ear, sharply and mutters something under his breath. I think the word in English is 'stupid'.

The hallway beyond Customs is massive but there are people enough here to wallpaper it. There's shouting and calling out, and hands and arms waving. I've got my hands full pushing the trolley with our luggage on it so I don't join Nonno in waving back, even though for a while there it seems like he's waving at random, maybe hoping to connect with someone.

"Anyone you know, Nonno?" I ask because there's meant to be some nephew of his, a Nicola most likely, coming to collect us. I sort of think it's a dumbass-question because Nonno wouldn't know what his nephew looks like in the flesh since he's only ever seen photos of him, and even then, not a recent one.

I'm about to suggest we amble off to the side somewhere and wait when a mountain breaks away from the crowd directly ahead of me and starts galloping our way.

It's a huge, fleshy mountain with a massive beard and curly salt-and-pepper hair.

"Zio Nicola!... Zio Nicola!"

The mountain can speak. Turns out the mountain is my Nonno's late younger brother's only son. I find out he's in his forties.

I think it's my ribs the mountain crushes first, then my shoulders, and then the back of my neck. I've never been embraced in so many ways by one human being before, not even when Nonna Rocchina was alive.

I do my best to steer the trolley behind Nonno and my newly introduced cousin Nicola Giovanni. The Giovanni bit is to distinguish him from Nicola Gennaro and Nicola Mario. Or that's what I think he tells me.

"There's been a little bit of a mix-up," Mount Nicola tells us as we stroll out into the warm Rome morning. "Someone forgot to check on the transport arrangements and the other minivan isn't coming."

*How many vans do we need?* I'm thinking. *What do they think me and Nonno are travelling with? An entourage maybe?*

"Then they can wait until it arrives," Nonno hisses.

*They? Who is they?*

I'm trying to figure out what all the stress is over when Nonno presses the palms of his hands together as though in supplication and says, "You think I don't know what you're all trying to do, Nicola?"

"*No, ti juro*." No, I swear, Mount Nicola answers. "It was all planned. I was coming in Eugenio's van, and Gaetano...You remember Gaetano, Tannucio Trenta's youngest son? He was coming in his own van. Problem is that the Trentas has to get to market this morning and need the van, so..."

This trip is going pear-shaped already, and we're not even out of the Rome airport yet. At least I can tell the kids back home I've set foot in Rome, even if Nonno puts us on the next return flight.

But right then things improve. I spot dimple-snob-quiet girl. She's with a lady, an old lady, a bit like my Nonno actually. And guess what? Dimple-snob-quiet girl is pushing a heavy trolley with their luggage on it, just like I am. No pointy-end-of-the-plane busboys here, no sir.

I wave faintly in her direction. Man, she's pretty. She doesn't see me because she's so obviously searching for a cab or a hire-car, maybe even a limo, to take her and the lady she's with to some posh Roman hotel.

"Zio, please understand," the mountain is pleading with Nonno Nicola.

"After all these years, I must drive into my own town with people I have chosen not to talk to in more years than I care to remember. Is that what you're asking me to do, Nicola?"

This must be serious stuff because Nonno is shaking his head and pressing his palms together and sort of throwing his arms about, all at the same time.

"Why don't we catch a bus?" I suggest helpfully, but I guess buses don't stop here because I get the same lame look from Nonno and his nephew as I got from dimples-snob-quiet girl on the plane.

"Nicola, there are no direct buses to the village," Nonno informs me. "And if anyone was going to be obliged to catch a bus it would be them, not us."

"So, we don't like them?" I ask rather flippantly because it all sounds melodramatic to me right now.

"You don't have an opinion on the matter," Nonno spits forcefully.

I've seen my Nonno upset before, heaps of times. Angry even, but he looks more than either upset or angry at this moment. Nonno Nicola looks sort of... scared.

"Nicola Alberti."

The voice comes behind me. Another relo, I think and turn, ready to get another massive rib crush or worse.

"Nicola Alberti! I don't believe it!"

Can you die from shock? I mean, does it happen in real life that people get such a shock that they expire right there on the very spot where they got the shock?

Because I should be dead.

The voice that greets Nonno Nicola is attached to an old lady who is attached to a trolley being pushed by dimples-snob-quiet-girl!

Yeah, I've died and gone to Heaven.

It's the strangest thing. Nonno Nicola turns white then red then white again, all in the space of a few seconds. And the old lady, for all her bravura greeting, isn't exactly jumping out of her skin with happiness. In fact, she doesn't seem too keen to get in the minivan with Mountain Nicola, but he somehow manages to convince her that it's the minivan or nothing. Well, not unless the pointy enders want to hire their own taxi for the four-hour drive.

And I realise how I know that the old lady isn't too enthused to see Nonno Nicola. It's all in the way she pronounced Nonno's name. I've heard it a million times at school. It's the tone that tells the receiver the greeter knows who you are but would rather they didn't. Or worse still, that the receiver gets out of their sight post haste—as in, Nicola Alberti, you're a dropkick!

It was like dimples-snob-quiet asking me if I was waiting to use the toilet on the plane. It was all about her, not me. She wasn't interested in me as much as she was interested in getting into the toilet first. I was an inconvenience.

I had just met Nonno's "they".

"Aurelia," Nonno says finally, then turns and lets Mountain Nicola lead the four of us to the one minivan.

There are clear blue skies above us. Not a single cloud yet it's freezing where I'm standing. Icy.

"I'm Nick," I offer when it's obvious no one is making any formal introductions, especially not Nonno Nicola who decides he'll ride in the passenger seat next to Mountain Nicola.

"Lia," Dimples-snob-quiet-girl says, but leaves my hand hanging in the air where I've stuck it out as though this is some business meeting.

*Nice name*, I think.

Turns out the old lady is Lia's Nonna. Not that Lia tells me exactly. I work it out from the conversation they have which excludes me...and Nonno Nicola. Maybe people who travel in the pointy end of the plane don't know how to strike up a conversation with normal people.

I guess it's up to me to break the ice here.

"So, how was the flight?" I start, then add, "I didn't see you guys board in Melbourne. Did you guys board separately to the rest of us?"

The moment I make that statement, I realise it's another bus stop moment and I cringe. Too late.

"We boarded in Brisbane," Lia answers flatly. "It was easier to do that since that's where Nonna and I live. Brisbane."

"Yeah, right. That makes sense."

*  *  *

Rome is dirty. Well, the outskirts anyway. Mountain Nicola doesn't do the tourist thingy and take us to have a quick peep of the Colosseum or the Vatican, or even a stray Roman ruin or two. No, he heads straight for the highway and south, past areas where there's nothing but high-rise buildings with washing flapping off of balconies, graffiti smeared along crumbling walls, and the occasional ancient aqueduct still standing in the middle of a vacant lot among dilapidated warehouses and petrol stations.

"This your first trip to Italy?" I ask when I've answered as much as I can of Mountain Nicola's questions about the flight, the state of soccer in Australia, and he's reassured me and Lia on what a great time it is to visit Castel Pulcinella Velato.

"First time to this part of Europe," Lia answers and continues to stare out the window.

"You've been to other parts of Europe then?" Like that's not an obvious assumption!

"Nonna Aurelia took me to Paris two years ago, and to London. She thinks a visit to her hometown would be interesting."

Lia speaks with a touch of aloofness. There's a kind of halting, semi-breathless quaver in her voice. I like it. I can tell by the way she made the last comment that, like me, she doesn't really think there's going to be too much excitement in this trip with the olds.

Hey, we have something in common finally. Well, that and the fact that we're both travelling with our own version of antiquity.

I'm just about to ask a few more probing questions when Lia whips out her phone, puts her really expensive earbuds in, and tunes me out.

And that's when I realise I've left my old iPod on the dresser in my bedroom in Melbourne.

"She's very tired," Aurelia tells me. "You should just rest. It's a long drive to the village."

"Still offering advice, I see," Nonno Nicola cuts in. "Even when it's not asked after."

Aurelia doesn't even look at Nonno Nicola. Instead, she gives a weak smile in my direction and offers me a boiled lolly from a small paper bag. I take the candy and pop it in my mouth before Nonno can tell me to chuck it away. Not that he does, but I'm figuring he might, seeing as how he seems to have this thing about this old lady.

*You two know each other well?* I think to ask, but don't. I grin sheepishly and narrow my eyes in Nonno's direction, sort of willing the question telepathically to him. But he's not receiving, or if he is, he's failing to transmit a reply. When I try to do the same to Aurelia, she has her eyes closed, head leaning against the window, hands folded on her lap.

And that's when I notice that she's wearing the most beautiful bracelets on both wrists, and her watch is one of those you see in expensive magazines. The very kind that people who travel in the pointy end of the plane wear.

Nonno Nicola wears the watch they gave him when he retired from the railways. It has a gold band and a crystal white face with Roman numerals. Nonno Nicola has willed it to me. I know because he's told me. It's our secret.

# CHAPTER SIX ~ Aurelia

Ugh! We finally make our way out of the airport onto the curb side. We wade through the hoards of people. There are lines, queues and more lines of people everywhere we go. Passport checks, customs and luggage collection. I spot the dorky guy a few times here and there. He is with an old man, obviously his grandfather. But never really close enough to say "hey".

"Who's picking us up, Nonna?"

"Gaetano," she replies, busy fluffing in her handbag. I have visions of a sleek white limousine gliding up to us, the door flowing open with the hottest driver in Italy ready to take our luggage and help us into our seats.

"Who's Gaetano?"

Nonna ignores me and looks over to her left. Her eyes squint like when she tries threading her sewing needle.

"Nonna?"

She walks off. *Huh?* She leaves me with all the luggage balancing precariously on the trolley. How embarrassing, standing by myself at the airport curb. Wait, what if Gaetano our limo driver arrives, and we aren't here? I run after her…Well, run? That's really not me. I walk fast to catch up with her. She stops near the geeky guy—I think his name is Rick. He is with the old man and another guy whom I couldn't care less about. They have their backs to us. The old man is pretty cranky, going off in Italian to the other guy, and Rick just sort of stands to the side and looks as confused as I feel.

"Nicola Alberti." The words just pop out of Nonna's mouth.

They all turn to see us stand there. I feel like an idiot. Nonna is being major embarrassing at the moment. She must think she knows them or something. Like, yeah, right. She doesn't even have her glasses on and like what are the chances of seeing someone you know the minute you land in Italy? But what happens next shocks me out of my embarrassment.

"Aurelia," the old, cranky guy replies, and not that happily, I notice.

He is wearing an old, worn belt that is probably from the seventies. And it would be classified as vintage... but not when he's wearing it! Wha-? They know each other? That's amazing. A few uninterpretable words are exchanged in Italian, and then silence as Nonna and the others head over to a minivan. Like, hello! Am I just another piece of luggage? What is going on? Where's Gaetano? Keep me in the loop please. I look at Rick and then find out his real name—he introduces himself as Nick.

"Lia," I reply but I am pre-occupied with what is going on as Nonna sits in the back.

"Nonna?" I lean into the van. "What's going on?"

"Aurelia, get in," Nonna replies stiffly.

"Is he Gaetano?" I point to the nameless guy.

"*Siediti!* Sit down!"

Oh nice. They tell me all my life not to get into vehicles with strangers and then my own grandmother is luring me into this rusty rundown minivan with three other men, and I have no idea who they are, they could be murderers, rapists or paedophiles, maybe all three!

"But Nonna..."

"Aurelia!" Nonna snaps. I can tell she doesn't want to ride with these people, so why are we?

Where are they taking us? Maybe we are hostages. Well, we did land in the middle of gangster land, Italian style. That might answer why Nick and his grandfather were on our plane, keeping an eye on us.

We sit in silence as we drive through Rome. I am with Nonna on a bench seat and Nick is next to me in a single seat. We have the aisle between us. Nick's Nonno is in the front next to the driver, whose name is Nicola, not Gaetano. Of course, the Nonno would sit in the front as if he were the 'boss'. He didn't say a word to Nonna. I don't get what it is between the two of them. I look out the windows. Rome! Where are the images that you see in glossy mags? All I see are dirty streets and dirtier old buildings.

Nick tries making conversation with me.

"*Gu* no talk to hims," Nonna whispers to me.

Huh? Don't talk to him? Why not? Then again, I am so jet-lagged and nauseated that I don't feel like talking anyhow. I can come across as snobby when I don't really know somebody that well. I sort of fade out of the conversation but am slyly checking out his dress sense. He isn't very cool, just wearing jeans and a t-shirt. It's his runners that kill him, death by runners, white runners, not the cool metro looking white runners but… white runners. I thought senior citizens were the only people who wear these types of white runners, then I peer over at his Nonno's shoes… white runners; they must have got two for the price of one. I know, I know, I am getting bitchy. I am super tired, and I don't want to have a convo with him, not right now, my head aches and I feel like I am having an out of body experience, so I mumble replies to his thousand questions then finally pop on my headphones.

Two hours later, I wake up as the van swerves around a corner… actually, *up* a corner. I find my head and nearly half my body over on Nick's side. Felt like the car had gone up on two wheels. This guy, Nicola, is driving like a nut. We keep going up and the road keeps getting windier. I start to feel sick. Where the hell are we?

Nonna has a sweet smile on her face, she looks so serene, no—maybe excited.

"We no far now, Aurelia," she whispers as my head and half my body swerve over to her side of the van. "Look," Nonna points to the top of a mountain. There, squatting like a duck on its nest, is a castle. A very old castle, but a real one! White and grey buildings are spotted below it. It looks surreal. I'd seen postcards of this village and the castle, but now I am close enough to take my own postcard photo.

I grab my phone and start snapping shots. I get one of Nonna's face with the castle in the background. A tear, a single tear, falls down her cheek.

"Are you okay, Nonna?"

"Shh, *si*, no worry," she whispers and then looks over at Nick's nonno whose face had also softened. I can tell he is trying to stay tough, just like what my Nonno Vito used to do.

One more bend and we cruise into a medieval looking town.

"*Siamo arrivati!*" announces the driver, Nicola.

"Castel Pulcinella Velato." Nonna and Nick's nonno say at the same time.

"Obviously we're here," Nick informs me.

I look at him. I can't believe we actually made it.

## CHAPTER SEVEN ~ Nicola

The rain is spritzing us as we climb but Nonno Nicola won't be talked out of it. He's very excited about today, like there's something special about climbing to the summit and visiting the chapel of the Madonna there. I'm not even over meeting the relos yet.

In the few days we've been here, I've met more Nicolas and Nicolettas than I ever imagined inhabited the earth at one time. It's kind of odd having so many people share your name. In Australia, it was just me and Nonno, but here it's like a plague.

Still, the food's great. The day we arrived, we had roasted rabbit, pork sausages, stuffed artichokes, preserved peppers, and patatelle—cheese balls in broth—just like Nonna Rocchina used to make. I saw Nonno Nicola get a little emotional at the table but not as emotional as he was when the minivan arrived in the village, and he saw his birthplace for the first time in so many years.

Nonno Nicola just stood by the minivan, swarms of people all around him, grabbing at him, hugging him, patting him on the back, and stared down this narrow street that he later told me led to his childhood house. The very house he took me to yesterday and had me film him as he walked through it and reminisced about the olden days.

I never knew until I heard him tell it to the camera that Nonno Nicola had been forced to hide in the attic of the house on more than one occasion when the local fascists had come looking for young boys to recruit into their ranks. Or that he had lost a younger sister, Carmelina, to tuberculosis when she had been just five years old, and that she had been laid out in her pine coffin before the funeral in the room that had served as both a kitchen and a bedroom, a simple light blanket serving as a dividing wall between the two areas.

I've been thinking about all this again and wondering where Lia had got to all morning. Since dropping her and her Nonna off in a small piazza where their relos had gathered, I haven't had a chance to catch up with Lia. Last I saw of her, she was following a woman who had popped a suitcase on her head and was making for a side street.

And it's not like this place is a city or anything. It's not even the size of a decent Australian suburb, so not seeing someone here is kind of weird. But then again all I've done in the past few days is eat, catch up on sleep from the jet lag, meet another cousin, *compare, comara,* or local sticky-beak come see what all the fuss is about.

But I haven't seen Lia. And Nonno is clearly not too keen on catching up for a yarn with the other foreigners because he hasn't even mentioned them once—well, not that I've heard anyway.

So, I'm trudging a short distance behind Nonno Nicola up this steep incline that is about as wide as a donkey's rear end. I'm trying hard not to think about how much further there is to climb and wishing that at least if Lia was here, too, I'd have someone to talk to apart from my cousin Raffaele who speaks English the way I speak Greek, with no grasp of the language at all. I've decided to call him Raff. He thinks it's an English equivalent of the Italian word for refined, *raffinato.* Dream on!

I wish Nonno had pulled someone else's name from the hat. Not really. I'm just bored. All we do is sleep, visit people Nonno remembers from before he migrated to Australia, have them visit us, eat as though we've been starved of food for a few months, and take walks through the village after dinner every night. And I have to do this while I'm arm-in-arm with one cousin or other, male or female it doesn't matter, it's just what they do here, parade along the one main street gawking at one another, stopping for a gelato or a granita at one of the many bars, and then repeating the process until it's time to head home.

And still I haven't seen Lia once. Maybe the pointy-end-of-the-plane segregation applies here too; posh people do *la passeggiata* at a different time to the *povos* like us.

"Nicola," Nonno calls and waves me to his side. "I have wanted to make this pilgrimage with someone I care very much about ever since I left my village," he says so softly I have to lean in to hear him. "I wanted to return here with your Nonna Rocchina, but time was against us. You understand, Nicola? Time cheated us. Time and place both."

I nod, but I don't really understand. Basic Italian is about my speed. This philosophical stuff is a bit beyond me, although I get the general drift.

Besides my cousin Raff, Mountain Nicola and his wife Adriana are with us. Adriana hasn't left Nonno's side all the while we've been climbing. Now though, she's standing off to one side as though she doesn't belong beside Nonno.

"Old men have old wounds to heal, Nicola," Nonno sighs. "And old women too."

I'm listening, sort of, but I'm looking past Nonno. At Lia. She's standing outside the little chapel with a group of girls her own age having her photo taken by one of them. She looks very serious. Even from here, I can see that she's frowning.

"Nicola? Nicola, are you paying attention to me?"

"What?"

Nonno Nicola huffs. He follows my eyes and shakes his head.

"Sorry," I whisper.

"The past is never a place we completely escape from," he says to no one in particular, but the words must mean something to Adriana and Mountain Nicola because they close ranks around Nonno and sweep him toward the chapel at a trot.

"You Nonno, he is paying for you come here?" Raff suddenly asks into my left ear. "I wish someone would pay for me to visit Australia. You have very nice girls there in Australia," he adds in Italian.

Raff takes me by the elbow and nods toward Lia. "Maybe you can introduce me to your Australian friend, yes?"

"Maybe," I reply. I doubt it though. Lia seems to be in a league apart from the one I'm usually invited into.

I don't get another word in when Raff has me hurtling in the direction of Lia and her group. Before I can pull up or twist aside, I'm almost on top of Lia.

"*Ciao*, Teresa," Raff says loudly to the girl handing Lia back her phone. "I'd like you to meet Nicola. He's from Australia." Raff holds my arm out so that my hand is extended toward Teresa. My eyes though are trying to communicate the message to Lia that this was not my idea.

Teresa takes my limp hand, shakes it then giggles and introduces each of the other girls—Assunta, Maria and her cousin Rosaria. "And this is Aurelia…"

"Lia," Lia cuts in and narrows her eyes at me like I'm the one arranging this embarrassing moment.

The introductions are awkward because Raffaele is a sleaze. He winks at Lia as though he knows she's been waiting for him all her life. Lia for her part presses her lips together and blows me away with, "Hey, Nicola, need to talk to you about that bus you were waiting for." When she threads her arm through mine and gives the others a quick wave, I almost trip over my own tongue.

"*Ci vediamo fra poci minuti, va bene,*" Lia breezes in Italian. We'll catch up in a few minutes, okay?

My cousin Raff offers to show us around, but Lia is quick and turns our backs to him, forcing Raff to defer whatever intentions he might have for another time.

The moment we're round the corner of the chapel Lia steps away.

"They're too much."

"Yeah, the rellies are overwhelming. Hey, you been down to the grotto?" I ask like it's the most intelligent thing to say. Not.

35

"Small doses," she utters, ignoring my question. "I can only take them in small doses. And who's the slime ball?"

"That'd be my cousin Raff…Raffaele," I whisper.

"Yeah, right. Figures." Lia steps away from me, brushes down her arms as though I might have left a stray scent on her, and adds, "Well, thanks for that." Then with a shake of her head, she strolls off.

*What is it with this girl?* I'm thinking and make as though to follow when suddenly Raff is on my heels.

"Your Nonno is looking for you," he tells me shortly. He's too obviously annoyed about 'missed opportunity' Lia.

I lose sight of Lia in the throng of people surrounding the many stalls that line the open square that surrounds the chapel. I find Nonno standing with Adriana and Mountain Nicola by a narrow entrance opening into the rear of the chapel.

"We go down together," Nonno informs me and before I can protest, I'm bundled down a metal ladder into a pit that finally ends in a dimly lit claustrophobic grotto.

It smells of undisturbed dust down there. Sort of cloying, like you've had too much chocolate. And it's cold, ice cold.

How Nonno Nicola makes it down the steps is beyond me, but he does, and stands next to me, his face a fold of dark shadows.

"This is where she was found," he announces. "Right here." Nonno points around the grotto, into the dark corners, at a raised rock ledge that has four short candles flickering on it beside photos of the Madonna in gilded gold frames. He makes the sign of the cross several times and nods as though his head has become too heavy for his neck to support.

As I stand there, Nonno, with some help from Adriana, fills me in on the by whom, how and when the statue of the Madonna was found in this grotto. Of course, I've heard it all before, many times, from Nonno, from Nonna Rocchina, from Mum even. But here, in the semi-gloom, with the walls of the place so close and personal, it sounds much more plausible than it did when the story was told to me around the lunch table in Nonno and Nonna's house in Melbourne.

Just as we climb out, I spot Lia again. She's with her nonna. They're in the queue waiting to descend into the grotto. Lia doesn't even look in my direction, but her nonna gives me a thin smile and a little wiggle of the head. It's as though she's saying, "Don't worry about my granddaughter, she's very shy." Yeah, as if I think that; I let Raff lead me to where Nonno Nicola buys us all a char-grilled pork sausage in a thick slice of homemade bread.

I need to catch up with Lia, I decide. She couldn't be too far. It's just not on that she acts like she's the catch of the day and I'm some scummy bait-size morsel that got trapped in the fishing net by accident.

"There's someone I want you to meet," Nonno says, grabbing me by the elbow and spinning me away from my intended path.

"I've got to be somewhere," I manage, but it's a pathetic whimper of a protest and Nonno Nicola knows it. He's paid for the trip. It was his idea to fly us to the other side of the world, and like Mum told me before we left Australia, "You do what Nonno asks. This trip must be very important to him, so don't you mess it up. Understand?"

"You want me to give that pretty girl a message for you?" Raff asks through a sly grin. His green eyes are laughing.

"No," I spit because the last thing I need is my sleazeball cousin using me as an excuse to get anywhere near Lia. Like she'd ever forgive me!

Raff must think he has a chance with Lia because right then he decides to leave me with the oldies and go back to the grotto.

*Yeah, good luck there, Raff!* I'm thinking when suddenly Nonno Nicola stops walking, and I plough into his back. He gives me one of those "Are you blind?" looks, and then shakes his head. Like maybe I'm a disappointment to him right now.

I decide to let Lia deal with Raff and focus on Nonno Nicola.

Good thing too, because just after he introduces me to the bloke with the folded, crippled, brown paper bag face, playing the piano accordion by a stall that's selling all manner of religious iconoclasm—got that word in RE class back in Australia actually—Nonno Nicola has a bit of a turn. He goes all pale, faint, and unsteady on his feet. We have to find a shady spot for him, and the bloke bashing the piano accordion gets Nonno some cold water. Adriana pours half down Nonno's throat and the rest over the back of his neck.

"Is he all right?" a voice asks, and I look up and see Lia's nonna standing there. "What happened to him?" I look, but I don't see Lia.

"He was introducing Nicola to Pasquale when he felt faint," Adriana explains.

Lia's nonna nods knowingly and looks back over her shoulder to where the Pasquale is again playing away on the piano accordion. "*Il Sacristan*," she mutters.

Sacristan? So, that must be like an altar-boy, helps with all things church like.

"He just sort of went funny when I reached out to shake the guy's hand," I offer in English as though that might explain everything.

Just then, Nonno kicks out gently with both feet and demands to be helped to his feet.

"You okay, Nonno?"

"It's the altitude," Nonno says crabbily. "I'm not accustomed to it any longer."

"The church isn't such a bad thing, Nicola," Lia's Nonna Aurelia says, but I'm not sure if she's talking to me or to Nonno. Either way, the comment is so random both me and Nonno exchange quick glances as I help him brush aside all further offers of assistance.

"He's okay. He's fine," I say and letting Nonno lean heavily on my arm. I lead us into the chapel where Mass is just about to begin.

I'm somehow not really surprised to see Lia and her nonna arrive and sit several pews back from us a few minutes later.

## CHAPTER EIGHT ~ Aurelia

Villa Racana sits on a hill just under the castle, overlooking the town. I stand on the balcony that flows from my bedroom and look at the beautiful view. I can see the castle ruins. Nonna's family are rich in Italy too. But Nonna sets me straight. Apparently, they weren't always rich—when she was a kid, they were poor just like the other farmers and villagers. Then her dad was one of the shrewd ones who discovered there was petrol close by, and that's how the family made their money.

"Everybody laughed at my father," she told me, "The day the gush come; they stop laughing!" Sounds a bit like Nonno Gerardo's story about the vineyard.

Staying in this village is like living in the dark ages. Cold showers! My uncle Antonio has to turn the hot water system on because I want to shower, apparently, they just wash themselves with a washcloth, and shower like once a month, eeew! Then his wife, Zia Santina, she is Nonna's sister so is my great auntie, collects two buckets of water every night. I am like, "What the...?" Well, apparently, the town water gets turned off every night so if you want water to drink, wash up or flush the toilets, you have to collect it for later. And I thought Italy was super modern; that's obviously just the fashions, not the plumbing systems!

We go for a *passeggiata* downtown, which is just walking up and down the main street; Nonna takes me by one arm and my cousin Rosaria by the other. The walk, or *passeggiata*, is what they do here every night after dinner. I just think it's gossip time for the oldies and perve time for the young people. The guys are such perves, all they do is stare, and I feel like saying, "Take a photo, it'll last longer!"

It's okay when the hot guys stare though. I notice the super-hot guy in town—he doesn't stare, well, not yet, he just glances my way and looks away when I glance back. He's always around when I'm going on one of the walks, which we seem to do all the time, but the main one is the night walk where everyone dresses up after dinner and goes out. It's like us going clubbing or to a party. Here they just walk and socialise, flirt and chat, but they're sober!

I don't see one speck of grass in the town; everything is cobblestone, concrete and brick—the road, houses, doorsteps, rooves, everything! Anything green is confined to the hills. We walk down the hill into town and all I can think of is the walk back up that same hill! We pass many a sight, and I don't mean touristy views or wonders of the world. I mean things like a goat tied up to a donkey, and the donkey was tied to a woman, all three trot off down one of the cobblestone passages on their way to wherever.

I feel like I am in some medieval town, or even one of those historical villages you visit in year five to study the gold rush. Everyone knows each other, like when we arrived yesterday in the town piazza, we were mobbed, and the whole town came to greet us, all of two hundred, shouting Nonna's name and Nick's nonno's name. There was hugging, crying, screaming and plenty of tears and then this old lady who looked double Nonna's age picks up my big heavy suitcase with its excess baggage, pops it on her head like a book and carries it up the hill!

Nonna starts with the same old story I've heard a million times, how she moved to Australia when she was seventeen, lived with some relatives and then met Nonno Gerardo yadda yadda. At least my cousin Rosaria, who is Zia Santina's granddaughter, is interested in the story...or pretends to be anyhow. I am so bored, bored and triple bored. There is no use watching TV; it's all in Italian and even though I can understand the language, the shows are crap. There's nothing to do here, no cinemas, no shopping centres, nothing. And the food is blech, they tried feeding me rabbit the other night, like, rabbit? Hello, I had one as a pet when I was a kid, you don't eat rabbits! It'd be like eating your pet guinea pig, and I'm told they eat them in Peru!

When they realised I wouldn't eat it, they tried telling me it was chicken. Whatever! And there's all this mushy bean and veggie stuff—I'd like to see whatever it was in original form, thanks. And pasta, pasta and more pasta. Carb city! That's why they are all a little podgy, can I have some protein please? But not rabbit! I wonder what Nick is eating, and what he is up to, even in such a small village I am amazed that we haven't run into each other yet, not even on *passeggiata.*

Nonna's *passeggiata* takes us through town and then up a hill on the other side, just under the castle. We are going to go visit a church or chapel where some statue of the Madonna was found like a thousand years ago. Like who cares—it's just a statue, it's not like it was a dinosaur bone or a human mummy!

On the way up, an old lady calls Nonna over to her.

"Wait here," Nonna gestures to Rosaria and me. It looks friendly at first as they kissed each other on both cheeks. Then voices are raised, and I think I pick up on a word or two, and then Nonna rushes back over to us. Her face is very red.

"What's wrong, Nonna?"

"No worry, stupid people in dis town," she says as she fans her face with her hand, "they have brains just like a donkey, no, even da donkey is smarter!"

"Did she say *bambino?*" I ask.

Nonna looks at me and doesn't answer.

"Nonna?"

"*Si, bambina…* she asks who you were." Nonna looks away, "I told her you are my *nipotina,* my granddaughter."

I know some Italian, Nonna has paid for lessons for about ten years now. *Bambino* is a little boy, not a little girl. Although when the oldies in this town talk to one another, they fall back into some ancient dialect, so sometimes I get it wrong.

I look back over to the other lady. She still stood there with hands on hips and a snide look on her face. I don't think Nonna is letting on to what the convo was about, but it didn't sound very amicable.

We finally reach the summit where the chapel is with the castle as its backdrop, it's quite pretty. There is a heap of people. Looks like it is some type of *festa*. Nonna had walked in silence the whole rest of the way after talking to that other woman. I wonder if Nonna is upset by the conversation or maybe just tired from the walk. I also think that Nonna planned this walk all along and just didn't tell me in case I pulled out. I'm sure if we'd stood at my balcony and she pointed to the summit on the other side there would be no way I would be here right now!

I notice that Nonna is mesmerised by the sound of an accordion playing. I look over and see the musician, he is old—well, not as old as Nonna, maybe like Uncle Vincenzo back in Australia, and wearing one of those long brown robes with a rope around his waist. Religious trinkets surround him. I urge her to go closer; maybe she wants to buy some of the merchandise. He has this sort of weird smile, you know those weird religious people who are happy with their own company, and sways from side to side as he plays—but then maybe he is on drugs.

"Pasqualino, *come stai*?" somebody asks as they walk past him. Nonna backs away. Her face changes like she's just seen a ghost. Well, he is a bit creepy looking.

"Lia," Rosaria calls me over to a group of girls who are apparently more of my cousins. Second, third, or fifty-sixth, who cares? Like I'm going to see them again after this trip.

They gather around me to take photos like I'm a celebrity, maybe they think I'm Tay Tay, except I am totally the opposite with my dark looks! So, if they are going to treat me like a celeb, I'll act like one! I pop my sunnies on and pose like Taylor. They then start to swarm me. I can't breathe.

"Hey," a voice from behind me. An Aussie voice. Ugh, Nick! Good timing, I guess. He reluctantly came over to introduce his cousin Raff, what kind of an Italian name is that? Anyhow, he is giving me the slo-mo once over with his sleazy eyes. I take Nick's arm and pull him aside to escape. Phew! I use him to take a breather.

"They're too much," I look away; don't want to give Nick eye contact, even though I feel a familiarity with having him around.

"Yeah, the rellies are overwhelming," he agrees. "Hey, you been down to the grotto?"

I ignore him and turn around to see my cousins with Nick's cousin all staring at us. Raff, the sleaze, winks at me. Like who winks nowadays, but sleazy guys standing at cheap bars, or somebody with a nervous twitch.

"Thanks for getting me away from them." I take my arm out of his. "Oh yeah, and by the way, apparently I'm not supposed to be talking to you," I add.

"Yeah, me neither," Nick laughs.

I step over to join Nonna who is waiting in line to go down to the grotto. The lineup is something to do with the Madonna statue; you go down these really steep steps to the grotto where the statue is stored. She crosses her arms and isn't very happy. Nonna that is, not the statue.

"I told *gu*, no talk to dat boy"

"Why not, Nonna?"

Nonna doesn't answer and then changes her mind about the grotto 'cause her knees are going to give in she says, thank goodness, like who wants to go down a dirty, old, cold hole with Italians in such a confined space all breathing stinky garlic and parmesan breath? And has anybody here heard of deodorant?

"Aurelia!" Nonna pulls me over to where a crowd has gathered and points to the ground. It's Nick's nonno. They'd just come out of the grotto and there he is, flat on the ground. He's collapsed, fainted or something. Just as well we didn't go down there if this is what happens to you! Maybe it's like one of those evangelist TV shows, where they touch you and you fall to the ground, maybe he is healed now.

Nonna stands over Nick's nonno and mumbles something about the church and I'm sure she says something about death; did she just wish he were dead? Like, nice, Nonna, the guy just collapsed, and you talk about the church and death.

Nick then rambles something about meeting the sacristan guy, but I don't know if he is rambling to me or to himself. I look over and there is the freaky sacristan guy still playing that stupid piano accordion again like nothing has happened. Maybe he is into witchcraft or something, and put a spell on Nick's nonno, who miraculously stands up with Nick's help. Nonna and he glare at each other. What is it with these two?

Nonna and I step into the church and sit a few pews back from Nick and his nonno. My stomach rumbles. It is way past lunchtime, and I am starved. All they have on the summit are homemade sausages in big chunks of bread, hmm, and that'd be good for me! Pork and carbs, not! Or is my stomach rumbling nervously? Sitting in church always makes you remember your guilts. Nonna still doesn't know my secret. Mum swore me not to tell Nonna, but I feel really bad, you know, with her paying for the trip and all.

Nick turns back to look at us, did he hear my stomach rumble? He's probably not such a bad guy, maybe I should be nicer to him, but why? And Nonna doesn't want me talking to him anyhow, but I might need him to get over the next week, you know, familiar face and all.

I look to my right and there along the church wall is that really hot guy staring at me. The one I keep seeing on the *passeggiata* walks. I sort of smile shyly and look down at my lap, look up again quickly and he's not doing his usually look away; he smiles and winks. Corny, yeah, and I just said that guys who wink are sleazy, but this guy is forgiven for winking 'cause he's too scorching hot!

## CHAPTER NINE ~ Nicola

I don't dare mention Nonno's turn to Mum. Not even when she asks me to explain in detail what's been going on, do I mention the episode up on the summit.

Instead, I mention the coincidence of there being another Aussie in the village at the same time as me and Nonno.

"People from the village migrated to all parts of Australia. All parts of the world, Nick," Mum says. "I'm surprised there aren't more Aussies there right now, what with the *Festa* and all."

We talk until the beep sounds three times, which means I've used up twelve minutes of credit on the phone card Mountain Nicola got for me so I could ring home.

As I hang up, I remember to tell Mum to give Dad a hug and to tell Danny she's missing out on a heap of fun. There's no way I'm telling her, or any of the others back home, that so far this trip is a total crash and burn—apart from Lia, of course, who I'd still like to get to know.

Raff is helping his oldies on their dairy farm this morning. One of the other cousins, Nicola Gianfranco, is on a bus to a morning market in a nearby town, and the other cousins are either too old or too young to have anything in common with me.

Raff had asked me to sleep over the night after the visit to the summit. He wanted me to bed in with him on the farm and have a go at milking their twenty cows first thing in the morning. Like that was always going to be fun—not! So, I've opted for leaving Nonno with some of his mates from the time of the dinosaurs, and come into the centre of the village, *la piazza*.

More and more stalls are appearing every day round the edges of the *piazza*, and all down the length of the main drag that leads out and into the village, in preparation for the official start of the

*Festa* in a few days' time. It's like a carnival without the mod cons around here now, and everyone seems totally excited by it all. If I wanted to, I could buy everything from nougat dipped in chocolate to metal bangles shaped to look like spiralling snakes. There's even a stall selling miniature replicas of the Madonna in wood, ceramic, pottery and glass.

Just before I phoned home, I almost bought a cool looking dagger that had red and green jewels embedded all along the handle, and a sheath that was the softest leather I've ever felt. That was until the chain-smoking stallholder tried to get me to buy a DVD of 'the much beautiful, sexy girls in the world' and refused to tell me how much the dagger was on its own.

When I said I was from Australia and wasn't travelling with a DVD player, the guy, who was about eighteen, tops, grinned. He pulled out a box from under the front seat of the battered van he was storing his gear in. and said, "No you worry, my friend," and shoved a mini-DVD player toward me with a price he said no one would dare meet or better.

I enter the Chiesa Madre, still grinning about the DVD and don't see the man standing just inside the doorway until I slam into him.

"Sorry," I say, pathetically. "*Scusa.*"

"*Bassa voce,*" the man replies. Whispers only.

I recognise him straight away. It's piano-accordion man. Except he doesn't have his instrument with him this morning. He's busy dusting the statues that line the back of the church, and he turns away from me without a second glance.

The church is small. It's in the shape of a cross, with the altar up one end on a raised platform. There are frescoes on the walls and ceilings, and against one wall, there's a glass case. I've heard about this case, and it's this I've come to see. Well, it's one of the things I've come to see.

There's a plaster replica of a saint's body in the glass case, laid out on its back and dressed in fading red and blue velvet robes. The arms are crossed at the chest and the saint is holding a martyr's palm. It all looks rather like a tattered haunted ride exhibition until I see what I've been told by Raff is the grimace on the plaster saint's face. The mouth is pulled back to reveal a row of teeth—real teeth, complete with brown stains and knobbly chips.

"Santo Benedetto," the voice at my back informs me. I look round and see the sacristan crossing himself. He's looking past me to the replica saint with the eerie grimace. "*Sono i suoi denti. Il corpo non esiste pui. Soltanto i denti.*"

I nod. I understand enough to know that he's just told me that the teeth are all that's left of the physical aspect of the saint. I also know from Nonno and Nonna that this glass case with the saint's teeth embedded in a plaster replica has been in the village church since even before they were born. Seems that every village in this part of Italy has the relic of one saint or another. Raff told me some of the larger churches have complete bodies. Yeah, interesting interior decorating.

Nonno sent money back to the village not long after Nonna Rocchina died. It doesn't take me long to find what his money was spent on. In a little alcove off to the right of the altar, there's a white statue of the Holy Mother. It's on a plinth and there's an inscription on a brass plaque that reads: "*In Memoria di Rocchina Alberti. Il marito, figli e nipoti.*" "In memory of Rocchina Alberti. From her husband, children and grandchildren."

There's a white rose at its base. Nonno Nicola made a point of bringing it the morning after we arrived, while I was still fast asleep with jetlag.

"Your grandfather is a good man, a very generous man," the sacristan's voice says at my left shoulder. He's standing beside me, looking at the statue of the Holy Mother. He's dressed in the same long brown robe he'd been wearing on the mountain—minus the piano accordion.

"You've come from Australia with Nicola Alberti. I know." Pasqualino touches the side of his hooked nose and gives a sly wink. "Don Francesco was very pleased to hear that he and Signora Aurelia were both coming back to the village for the *Festa*."

Because he speaks slowly, I catch most of what the sacristan says to me in Italian. I can't answer him clearly with words, so I nod again and putting a hand on my chest, tell him my name—which is stupid since I'd already been introduced to him on the mountain the afternoon Nonno had his turn.

But I do get one question out: "Why was Don Francesco so keen for my Nonno to come here?"

The sacristan smiles and motions for me to follow him. I do. He takes me to the back of the altar, through a narrow opening between it and the brickwork of the church's rear wall. There he points at another grotto, this one opening under the altar itself.

At first, I don't see much save for a mound of dirt and a few electric candles that are burning brightly. Then I see the gold box, about the size of a shoebox. I struggle to read the embossed writing on it. The sacristan sees my hesitation because he translates the words for me: "For the keeping of those children whose parents are unknown or unknowable," he whispers.

When I look at him in surprise, he adds, "I learn little bit English."

It's a collection box. The sacristan holds it up for me to look more closely at it.

Pasqualino shakes it near my ear. The box is empty. Then he touches the box and his own chest, repeatedly.

"This box is for you?" I ask. "You're… one…of these children. Or you were. Is that what you're telling me? You're one of the children…" I refer to the writing on the box. "You're one of the children whose parents are unknown or unknowable? The parish collects money for you at Mass, right?"

The smile the older man gives me is brilliant in its joy at the fact

48

that I seem to have understood him.

Then the sacristan points at a smaller inscription on the bottom of the collection box.

It reads: Nicola Alberti and Aurelia Racana.

My head does a snapping motion, like I imagine it would if someone like Lia were to give me a slap on the side of the head for daring to ask her on a date.

*Ka-pow!*

I reach out and touch the gold-coloured box. It's cool to my fingertips, but so smooth it feels like solid silk.

Then it hits me. With so many Nicola Albertis in this village, the name on the collection box could belong to any one of them. But it doesn't. I know it doesn't because I know two things for fact; firstly, it's no secret in our family that Nonno Nicola has always sent money back to his native village, and secondly, the sacristan said specifically that my Nonno is "a good man, a very generous man" just before he showed me the box.

I stare at the collection box. Of all the weird things I expected to see in the Chiesa Madre, this was certainly not one of them.

A thought presses into my mind.

Why, if Nonno Nicola has donated this collection box to the church, and he has been sending money back to help fill it, isn't Nonna Rocchina's name there beside his, but Lia's Nonna's is?

Nonno Nicola never did anything without Nonna Rocchina. Ever.

This is too weird.

I'm about to ask the sacristan the question when the sounds of voices in the church proper distract him and after putting the collection box back in its place, he indicates we should leave.

He stops me just as we pull ourselves to our full heights and says, "I'm very happy you have come to Castel Pulcinella Velato. I have heard so much about you, and Australia. Your Nonno writes beautiful letters to Don Francesco." He lowers his voice and a frown shadows his face. "He always reads the letters to me. And Signora Aurelia's letters too… I have trouble reading. It's not a gift I have."

"How old are you?" I find myself asking.

"*Sessanta questa settimana. Domenica della Madonna,*" the sacristan replies proudly. Sixty this week. On Sunday, the Madonna's Feast Day.

I blink. Not because there's the sun in my eyes or anything, but because I'm startled. It's like someone has tossed a rock into the placid waters of my life and created waves I don't really understand.

To make matters even more confusing, I bump into Lia and her nonna as I head out the door.

"Nicola," Lia's Nonna says like I need to be told who I am, but apart from a quick nod, I don't stop, not even when Lia herself calls my name.

## CHAPTER TEN ~ Aurelia

Hey, real weird, I am at the church again with Nonna–don't ask why, I don't understand anymore why we go there so much, whether mass is on or not, she is attracted to it like a magnet! Wants to sit in the pews for hours. Anyhow, we are about to walk in when Nick rushes out, nearly bowls us over. He looks like he is about to throw-up; wonder what made him sick. Might be that half-decayed body in there they call a saint.

"Nick," I call as he rushes off, but no response. Nonna elbows my ribs and glares. Yeah, yeah, don't talk to him, I get it. Italians are great talkers but sometimes they don't have to say a word and you still understand what they are trying to say.

We enter the church and it's funny, you know, 'cause Nonna goes all serene and angelic. Maybe I should carry around a miniature of the church and whenever she cracks up, whip it out and it'll calm her instantly. The church is empty; well, I thought it was until I see a dark shadow emerge from behind the altar down the front. The piano accordion guy, the creepy guy, he looks really scary now with his brown robe–like a zombie emerging from its muddy grave. Maybe that's why Nick rushed off—the guy scared him. Or maybe he's a paedophile.

Creepy, weird, paedophile guy smiles at us. Nonna gestures back and her serene, angelic face bleeds tears. Not sad tears but looks to me like happy ones as if she is in a place she's always wanted to be. I wonder what this church means to her. Why does she come here all the time? What draws her here? And why was Nick there, and on his own?

Anyhow, on our way back home, we walk through the town and notice all the stalls being set up.

"*La Festa*," Nonna tells me. The town is preparing for its festival religious thingie, where they carry a statue through town up to the church and then celebrate with stalls, food, drink and a carnival. Stalls sound good; I could do with some shopping. Although markets aren't my usual shopping scenes, I am desperate! I haven't bought a thing. There's one clothes shop and one shoe store. And they aren't that customer-friendly either. They don't like you to browse, and I found that out the hard way.

I'm in the clothing store with Rosaria, my cousin, and doing my usual, "Oh, this is nice," taking it off the rack, when Rosaria starts to look nervous. Then the shop lady comes over, grabs the hanger out of my hands, and puts it back without saying a word. Rosaria runs out embarrassed, and I walk out in a huff and whined to Nonna.

"Is different here, Aurelia," Nonna explains. "You walk in and know exactly what you want and dey get it for you."

Huh? Know exactly what I want? Oh, I'd like a blue skirt with pink flowers in size ten, you got one? Yeah, right. Shopping is like fishing: you throw your line in and you don't know what you are going to catch or like shell collecting. You don't go to a beach with a list, oh I want an oval shaped blue shell and nothing else. You go to the beach and walk around, browsing all the shells and pick up the ones that attract you. Same with shopping. I go shopping to relax and get excited. When I see something cute, then I can try it on, etc. Stuff shopping in Italy, well, Italian villages anyhow.

I don't even bother going into the shoe store, because if I don't go in with "Oh, I'd like a black pair of pointy shoes with straps," they'll kick me out! The markets are looking good, so when is Nonna going to take me *real* shopping?

Mum rings just after lunch, it's late back home, nearly bedtime. I hate to admit, but I think I miss her, I miss Sara, I miss everything about home, except—well, I'll have to deal with that when I get home. I get all the gossip about what is going on back home from

Mum, you know, local news and stuff. Sara keeps me up to date with messaging. Sara said there is some gossip about me going around among my peer group, saying I'd run away to live in Italy, whatever, or that I was in Italy because I was avoiding stuff.

I'm a bit bored so I ask Rosaria to look at photo albums. You know, photos of Nonna when she was young, her family and stuff. It's all a bit repetitious, people standing stiffly, not smiling at the camera; photos of donkeys, picnics, and hay and farm stuff. Nonna was right, they *were* poor; you could tell by their clothes and the depressed look on their faces. One photo falls out of the back of an album as I pass it back to Rosaria. It's a small photo, about the size of a school portrait for your wallet.

"Nonna?" I ask Rosaria.

"*Sì.*"

It's a photo of Nonna when she was about my age, but who was the guy? He had his arms around her, and it was obvious they were together. Didn't look anything like Nonno Gerardo, and she'd met him in Australia anyhow, didn't even look like her brother, not that it particularly looked like a brotherly hug either.

"*Chi e?*" I point to the guy.

"*Non lo so,*" she nods, she doesn't know either.

I have a closer look. The guy's face is familiar, I'm sure I've seen him before, but how? The photo is ages old, has to be over sixty years old if she's a teen in it. Who is he? Zia Santina walks in, squints at the photo in my hand, snatches it before I can say, "Smile for the camera" and pops it down her top, tucking it into her bra.

"Nonna!" Rosaria exclaims.

"Zia!" I say, "*Chi e?*" Maybe she knows who it is. No reply.

"*Io chiedo a Nonna.*" I get up from my seat, I will ask Nonna.

"No!" Zia screeches, "*Le cose del passato sono ormai dimenticati.*" Things that have passed are now forgotten. She just fuels the mystery even more. Who is this guy that Nonna was with that I'm not supposed to talk about? There's lots of 'don't talk to this person, don't talk about that person' going on in this house.

That night I have trouble getting to sleep. I go out onto the balcony and look across at the spot-lit chapel. It does look beautiful at night, especially with the shadow cast from the castle. The photo comes to mind again and I wonder what story that photo tells. There is a light knock on my door.

"Rosaria," I gesture for her to come in. She declines and hands me a photo, then slips away down the dark corridor. The photo. Rosaria must have snuck it from her nonna while she was asleep. I turn on the lights and stare once again at the faces. I know the girl is Nonna, but who is the guy?

He looks like…

Nick! The guy looks like Nick, the Aussie Nick, the Nick who's in town, geeky guy. Huh? Maybe it's just a coincidence 'cause Nick can't be nearly seventy years old…

This isn't making sense.

But hang on …

His grandfather is nearly or is already seventy years old.

Nick's nonno.

The guy in the photo is Nick's nonno!

## CHAPTER ELEVEN ~ Nicola

"What can I tell you, Nicola?" Nonno Nicola says when I ask him about the collection box. He's not looking me in the face as he speaks.

"How about you start with why you and Lia's nonna have your names on that box and Nonna Rocchina doesn't."

I look at Nonno. It's taken me most of the day to work up the courage to ask him but now that I have, I'd like an answer. There's some weird stuff going on that I don't understand, and even for me, that's something.

When it's apparent Nonno hasn't anything to say, or rather he *won't* say anything, I turn to Mountain Nicola. He's been here all along. He hardly ever leaves Nonno's side. It's like he's Nonno's personal bodyguard—which is also just more weird stuff.

I lift my shoulders at him, as though repeating the questions to him.

"An intelligent man is one who knows what he's talking about," Nonno says suddenly. "A smart man is one who knows when not to speak."

When I look back at Nonno, he's on his feet, his eyes narrowed, both hands on the pummel of the walking stick he's been using the past few days. It used to belong to his dad. We'd found it still leaning behind the door of the main bedroom in Nonno's childhood house when we'd visited.

"What?" I manage.

Mountain Nicola is busy with his head all of a sudden, shaking it and nodding and generally looking like he's covering something up. Something Nonno doesn't want me to know about.

"Does Mum know about the collection box?" I ask out of nowhere in particular.

55

"That Don Francesco," Nonno mutters, "There was no need to put our names on the blessed thing. No need at all." Nonno pushes his reading glasses up the bridge of his nose, three times in quick succession. "There is just no sense with these people. No sense at all…" Then Nonno points a finger at me and snaps, "Who did you talk to about the collection box?"

"No one apart from the old guy who looks after the church, the one who was playing the piano accordion on the mountain, he showed it to me. And he was really proud of it, too. He said the collection box was for people like him, whatever that means."

"Who else was there with you?" Nonno asks.

"*Nessuno.*"

"It wasn't Don Francesco. It was Don Donato, the priest before Francesco. He thought he was doing you a favour by engraving your name on the collection box," Mountain Nicola whimpers.

"*Silenzio!*" Nonno snaps and I blink in surprise. My nonno hardly ever raises his voice.

"You must forget the box, Nicola," Nonno says. "The box is nothing."

*Yeah, right.* The collection box is nothing. The collection box is something, all right. And I'm starting to think this coincidence of meeting up with Lia and her nonna here in the village, well, I'm starting to reckon this isn't much of a coincidence at all.

Raff has the hots for Lia, so when I suggest he shows me where the Racana house is, he nearly falls over himself with excitement.

"She pretty girl, yes," he tells me about a hundred times as we follow the narrow winding streets uphill. "You ask to her if she like come…" He gets stuck for words, so he waves me over to one side of the street and through an opening between two houses points toward the paddock at the bottom of the main road. A carnival is being set up there for the weekend festivities.

"You want me to ask Lia to go with you to the carnival, the rides?" I ask and use my hands to mimic driving a dodgem car.

Like that is ever going to happen. Lia agreeing to go to the carnival with Raff, I mean. Raff is a shepherd by trade. Lia is a professional shopper. Perfect match... not!

"My friends are having a party tomorrow night," Raff announces. "Of course you're coming... with me..." He grins sheepishly. I understand.

*"Tu vuole io invitare,* Lia?" I say in my very poor Italian. You want me to invite Lia?

Raff laughs and drops an arm around my shoulders. What is it with these guys and walking around with their arms around each other? Even when a group of Raff and his mates take me for the *passeggiata* in the evenings, at least one of them wants to drop an arm over my shoulders! It's like they're either trying to protect me or get it on with me. More weird stuff.

Castel Pulcinella Velato is a village built on two hills, one a lot bigger yet lower than the other. The Racanas, it seems, have their family home on the higher hill, the hill with the outlook toward the sprawling valleys as well as the sacred mountain. There's a castle just over its far wall! Not a big castle. It's crumbling and sort of leaning to the left, but it has battlements and ramparts, and stuff built into it.

Raff and his mates have brought me up to speed on who lives where. The people whose families have traditionally worked the lands have houses on the lower hill, and of course, there's a pointy-end-of-the-plane here too, and it's the higher hill where the landowners have traditionally lived.

I know enough about my family's past to know that we've always worked the land, never really owning enough of our own to make a go of being self-employed. Even Raff is a shepherd-for-hire. He left school at age eleven and never went back. He told me there was no point in getting a higher education since he had nowhere he wanted to go and nothing much he really wanted to see outside of the surrounding district.

"*Ecco la Villa Racana*," Raff announces, and I look up to see what for this region is a fancy house. It's set at the end of a short driveway behind a low wrought-iron fence whose two gates are open to allow the massive black dog to patrol just out into the street as far as its chain allows.

There are fig trees and lemon trees everywhere. There are even a few chestnuts, and a scattering of well-tended vine trellises all the way up to the house proper. Imposing? Yeah.

The dog barks loudly as we approach.

"*Basta!*" Enough, Raff barks back and tosses the dog a chunk of bone he's had concealed in his trouser pocket. He winks at me. "*Mi conosce.*" The dog knows me.

Raff laughs and leads me past the snuffling dog and to the steps that lead to the front door. He nods in the direction of the door then takes a step back arms limp at his sides.

I notice he has his head slightly bent too, as though not wanting to make eye contact with whoever might come to the door. I shake my head. It's as though the village has a sub-life all its own, with all sorts of real and imagined boundaries. I've noticed it in the shops too, where certain people just waltz in and, no matter how long others have been waiting to get served, they get immediate attention.

"Come here," I urge Raff in Italian, but he wiggles a finger at me and stands his ground. I can't understand this. He wants to go out with Lia, but he won't come to her door, or at least, her family's door. Like I said, weird.

As it turns out, Lia isn't home. It's one of the girls from the mountain, Rosaria, her cousin, who opens the huge wooden door.

"I tell Aurelia you come here," she smiles. Then she looks past me at Raff. I don't get all she says to him in Italian, but I get the gist of it. Something like, 'She's a city girl, Raff, don't get your hopes up.' And then she adds the strangest thing; "History doesn't always repeat itself, Raffaele."

For his part, Raff merely shrugs and turning away, ambles back toward the dog. I make to follow but Rosaria pulls me up short.

"Aurelia tells me you two met on the plane for the first time. Seems to me that your Australia is too big, even for family."

I see Rosaria narrow her eyes, staring past me over my left shoulder... at Raff. He's quick but not quick enough to hide the look of startled annoyance on his face.

"What?" I ask in a tinny voice of bewilderment. "What are you talking about?" I manage in Italian.

But suddenly Rosaria doesn't want to talk. She fusses with the strands of hair about her face and steps back into the house.

"Raff, what's she on about?"

"How would I know?" Raff mumbles and starts back toward the gate and the main road.

I don't know how he'd know, or even what he'd know, but I know that Raff knows something that I don't. And Rosaria knows it too.

Raff takes me to the *Gran Bar*, one of three street bars in town. Despite all my promptings, he insists he knows nothing about what Rosaria meant by her comment.

We drink lemon granitas and work our way through several helpings of delicious pizza made with a thin crust and just a shaving of cheese and oregano. In time some of his mates join us. They wander in from the odd jobs they do, everything from water wardens portioning out water for irrigation to the local farms, to fire-watch shifts on the fire tower out on the sacred mountain spotting for any potential outbreaks.

"You come with us to party, yes, Nicola?" the water warden asks.

"*Si che viene*," Raff replies on my behalf. Of course he's coming. "*Ha invitato* Aurelia."

"I haven't asked Lia yet," I correct Raff. "She wasn't at the villa, remember."

Raff laughs. He tosses back his head and shows his cavities. There's something manic about him that disturbs me slightly. He has a frayed edge—like the kids back in school who are just too cool for their own good.

"It's a big party, Nicola," Raff tells me and lights up a cigarette one of the others offers him. "You can't come all the way to Castel Pulcinella Velato and not come to the party. Everyone is going to be there."

"Hey, you bringing that idiot Pasqualino again this year, Raffaele?" one of the older guys tosses up into the midst.

"Why should this year be any different?" one of the twins who works as a mechanic for the local Agip agency pipes up. He's one of the cool guys all the girls hunger over. Tanned, toned, and dark. Yeah, a bit like me—if you really use your imagination.

The attention seems to shift to Raff, and everyone urges him to answer the question. Like he would know.

"He's harmless," Raff says finally through lips that are pressed tightly together, and not just because he has a cigarette burning there either. "Leave the poor guy alone. He doesn't do us any harm. And besides, I didn't bring him, okay."

Raff looks at me, and then when I catch his eye, he looks away.

The others all laugh in unison, but not Raff. Raff is looking down at his fingers where they drum on the tabletop.

"This Australian girl," Agip agency says suddenly with a drool. "I see her on the *passeggiata* with her cousin Rosaria and some more girls. You think maybe you can fix for her come to party, Nicola?"

*What is it with these guys?* I've hardly spoken a hundred words to Lia. How am I supposed to invite her to a party I don't even know if I'm going to yet?

"Yeah, sure thing," I answer like it's a done deal.

## CHAPTER TWELVE ~ Aurelia

I wake up with a headache, too much thinking, not enough sleep. The photo is really getting to me. I add a couple of paracetamols to my breakfast and slump at the table to drink my café latte, which of course isn't anything like the 'lattay' you get in cafes back home.

"Whatsa wrong with you?" Nonna walks in.

"Headache," I mumble.

"*Mal'di testa?*" she yells.

"Yes, Nonna, headache," I signal for her to keep her voice down.

"*Santina!*" Nonna yells for her sister. I groan. They mumble to each other in some dialect. Suddenly, Zia Santina grabs my head from behind and starts doing this gypsy-voodoo crap, rubbing my temples, forehead and muttering some devilish tongue language. I try to look back at her face, and just catch a glimpse of her with her eyes shut when she whips my neck back around into place. What the hell is going on? It's just a headache, what would they do if I broke a leg? Zia then stops dead, her hands go limp, and she lets out a big sigh and slumps down into a chair nearby.

"What the hell, Nonna?"

"Aurelia, she removes the curse."

"What curse?"

"The curse that make you head ache."

Curse? Aren't headaches caused by tension or food allergies or scientific medical reasons? Curses?

"Who put the curse on me?" I am curious.

"Bad peoples, jealous peoples."

Bad and jealous peoples. I'm over it, I've heard enough. They are pretty behind and backward in this village, they still believe in curses, they believe in witches, they believe in evil spirits. *Mum! Get me out of here!*

61

I finish my breakfast in silence and have to admit the headache has disappeared, but not from Zia's curse-dance but from the tablets, I am pretty sure.

I am trying to work out a good time to ask Nonna about the photo, but only once Zia disappears as she has already confiscated it from me once. I'm pretty sure it is Nick's nonno in the photo with my nonna and I want to know why. Finally, Zia Santina is heading out the door to get some eggs or something from their mini-market garden in their backyard.

"Nonna, I found this photo yesterday," I say, pulling the photograph out of my jean pockets.

Nonna takes the photo from me and squints at it. She then pops her glasses on and peers closely. She is pale, very pale.

"Aurelia, why you do this to me?" Nonna whimpers, drops the photo onto the table and puts her head in her hands.

"But, Nonna, who is he?"

"Nuthink. Nobody."

"Is it Nick's nonno?" I pause. "Signor Alberti?"

She looks up at me, her eyes glassy; she looks terrified. I feel sorry for her. I don't want to cause her pain or grief. I just want to know the truth.

"Aurelia!" Zia Santina calls from the door, and mutters something about helping her with the eggs.

"Si, Santina," Nonna gathers herself, stands up and heads to the door. I grab the photo before Zia comes back in. They both walk back into the kitchen with fresh eggs in their hands. Nonna can't look me in the eyes. I think it's time for me to give her some space; she obviously doesn't want to discuss anything at the moment, and it makes her really sad. I know how it feels, when you don't want to talk about something, and people are pushing you for answers.

Now I know for sure my nonna has a secret from her past that I want to uncover. Maybe her secret has impact on Dad, and then on me. But how can I do this without needling at Nonna for more information. Rosaria doesn't know much, only that there is this big secret, and nobody is allowed to talk about it. And it has something to do with Nick's family because both families don't talk to each other just like the Montagues and the Capulets. Maybe Nonna is Juliet and Nick's nonno is Romeo. And it's like there's an inter-village war going on, people are siding with each family, like that lady who had a go at Nonna the day after we arrived. So, I need to reveal more of this secret. But who can help me? Mum? I'm guessing she knows nothing. She's as in the dark as I was a week ago.

Nick? If this is Nick's nonno in the photo, maybe he knows something that I don't. Maybe Nick knows their secret, or maybe he's a mushroom as well, kept in the dark.

I have to show Nick the photo, and then maybe he can confront his grandfather and get more information that way.

I take the opportunity to sneak out of the house without having to explain myself while everyone is in the mini-market garden out the back picking veggies for lunch. The thing is that I have no idea where Nick is staying. So, I head down into town where the markets are set up, along with skeleton carnival marquees and rides behind a side street. Everyone is looking at me in a funny way, like 'why aren't you with your nonna?'

I just nod, smile and keep going, but I have no idea *where* I am going! I decide to brave the shoe shop and ask in my best Italian, "*Dov'e* Nicola?" Oh, God, then I realise I don't know Nick's surname! That'll teach me for not being interested in other people. The shoe shop lady is very patient, different to what I had imagined—a monster with two heads who ate you if you didn't buy a pair of polka dot purple shoes, size six exactly. I thought she might be mean like the dress shop lady, but she smiled and waited. "Nicola... bloody hell!" I let out in English.

"*Non so dove trovare,* Nicola Bludell," she looks puzzled. I had a little laugh, she doesn't know where Nicola Bloody Hell is, ha, neither do I.

*"Lui vieni dall'Australia."* He's from Australia, I explain.

*"Aha, si*—Nicola Alberti!" It was so draining I nearly collapse to the ground with exhaustion. She kindly points down the main street, and then makes lots of hand gestures, left, right, up, down, skew. On my way out, I thank her and take note to pop in again as I spot a gorgeous pair of soft pink leather flats that would go perfect with... anyhow back to Nick's nonno. I just head the way the shoe lady pointed, along the cobblestone paths and at least now I know his surname. I keep asking along the way for Nicola Alberti.

I approached the old wooden door that hooks to its stone frontage with medieval looking hinges. I'm about to knock but drop my hand and step back. What was I here for? What was I going to say? I reach into my back pocket and feel the photograph. At least I have some hard evidence, so Nick won't think I'm stupid. I reach up again and, as I was just about to hit the door with my knuckles, it swings open, and I nearly hit the old man on his nose.

*"Si,"* he grumbles.

*"Ah, cé,* Nick," and then I remember the nonno was from Australia and understands English. "Is Nick here?"

"No!" He frowns and is about to slam the door in my face.

*"Scusa,"* I take a tiny step forward. "It's important; I need to talk to him."

"He no here! And you no speak to him!"

Nonno Alberti really doesn't want me to see or talk to Nick. I get the family feud stuff, but we are like three generations away from all the fighting.

*"Chi cé?"* a voice from behind bellows and emerges from behind the nonno's head. He is so big his body also emerges from behind. It's like he is the nonno's bodyguard.

I know I am taking a risk, but I pull out the photo and show him.

"Is this you?"

Nick's nonno's face turns dark, not red or white, but dark—he is mad.

"*Via!* You go!" he screams at me. "Go to your family and tell them to not play the games with Nicola Alberti!"

Suddenly, the big guy steps out from behind Nick's nonno, rambles rudely in dialect and shoos me away like I am a low life or a beggar. I guess he *is* the bodyguard.

Well, there is no chance of talking to Nick if his nonno reacts like that. Actually, why *does* he react like that? That obviously is him in the photo. He just gave himself up, 'cause, if it isn't him, there is no reason for him to react so nastily.

I head home in despair and walk past the Gran Bar, the local café. I need a coffee, need to wake up my brain, work out what's going on. An espresso will do that. I go in, stand at the bar, and order my caffeine shot.

Moments later, my silence is disturbed by a bunch of guys talking loudly sitting at a couple of tables near the back door. I hadn't noticed them when I came in. One of them is Nick, another his sleazy cousin, a few others, and the hot guy, the hot, toned guy, the hot, toned, tanned, dark guy, with a cigarette that hangs precariously out of his mouth. Wow, he looks a little like an Italian James Dean, a dark James Dean. In Year Ten, we had to do a drama assignment about actors who died before their time. I did mine on James Dean, didn't have a clue who he was until then. James was hot, dead now but hot. This guy is alive and hot! I have to stop drooling, or I'll have coffee stains on my clothes.

It's not a good time to approach Nick, not with the pack of wolves all sitting there. Rosaria told me Italian café bars aren't really meant for women; that wouldn't stop me, but I don't want Nick and the others to see me, so I pay and aim for the side door so I can just sneak out. They haven't seen me, or so I think.

James Dean suddenly gets up and floats over, only because he looks like a god and gods float.

"*Ciao, bella,*" he's standing pretty close.

"*Ciao,*" I answer, but I can tell I'm blushing, not that he would be able to tell 'cause I have olive skin, but I can feel the heat rising into my face.

"*Io sono,* Marco." He holds his out his hand. I shake it and shyly leave him staring at my back as I head out the side door. As soon as I'm out, I lean against the wall; my heart feels like I have just run a marathon. His name is Marco, and I will be his slave, I will do anything he wants, but I can't let him know that, play it cool Lia, just like with the guys back home, play it cool.

When I get home, Rosaria tells me that Nick had just been to visit. We've obviously crossed paths. I wonder why he was visiting me, and I wonder if he saw me in the bar as I was leaving. I have to work out a plan to meet up with him, now that I have this generational secret to share. And what is the secret? Maybe we don't want to know. Were my nonna and Nick's nonno really lovers?

Nonna is real cranky at breakfast. Grumbly and bitey, just like a vintage cheese.

"You know, Aurelia, you should look at you own business."

Wha-? What business? Before I can open my mouth to defend myself—

"You spoiled and very disrespectful to your old people." Then she starts to cry for no reason. I mean, she probably has a reason, but I can't see one right now. What the hell? What has gotten into her?

"Where is dat photo?"

"What photo?" I play dumb.

"*Madonna, Gesu Christo!*" She is pissed, and as she stands up, she shakes the table and the milk spills onto the cloth and over the sides. Zia Santina rushes in, grabs a sponge on her way to the table. She calms Nonna down and glares at me.

"*Va lavarre i piatti*, Aurelia," Zia shoos me off to the sink to wash the dishes.

They sit at the table and mumble with lowered voices. I can

just grab snippets of words, bambino, Nicola, *chiesa*—baby, Nick's nonno and the church.

I get dressed and go out onto my balcony to get away from everyone. It is so serene as I gaze at the castle in the distance,. On a clear day it looks like a painting.

The front door slams, and I look down to see Nonna shuffle towards the front and down the road. She is going at a pretty fast pace for an old lady; I've never seen Nonna move like that. Where is she going? I consider just calling out for her to wait, so I could join her, but she obviously wants to be on her own, so then, I think, I have nothing to lose by following her.

I dash out and stay a good fifty metres behind her. She never looks back, so I'm not that worried about her seeing me—old people usually never look back: they are pretty focused. She is winding her way up the cobblestone paths. I work out she is heading to the church. That church! Again! How many sins has she committed to have to visit it so many times? Maybe she feels bad because we had a fight and wants to talk to the priest about it.

Nonna finally reaches her destination, under the shade of a huge fig tree just outside the church. Maybe she's tired and resting; it was a big walk, If I had known it was going to be the church she was heading for, I would have changed my shoes to a more suitable pair for walking! Anyhow, she stands there for a few minutes before she is disturbed by somebody coming up the path. It's Nick's old man, I mean old nonno! Crap, there is going to be a brawl. A Montague and Capulet blood shedding standoff. Can't believe the timing, like, you couldn't have planned it that way, the two of them there at the same time. Well, maybe they did plan it, from what I see next.

Nonno Alberti heads straight for my nonna. At first, I think he is about to have a go at her, even hit her, but instead they greet each other with an Italian kiss, both cheeks, and wait for it… a smile.

Huh?

Like what the…!

Aha, this is real Romeo and Juliet stuff, the families are at war, but the lovers still meet—lovers, at their age. Blech.

I'm not allowed to even look at Nick without Nonna giving me one of her twisted pinches to my thigh that feels like a hot steel rod piercing my skin, and there she is greeting Nick's grandfather like they are family. But they're not there for long before the priest comes out. A happy priest shakes their hands, and they follow him back into the church. Not into the main area, through a side door. My mouth is still hanging open in surprise when I notice somebody else spying on them across from me.

Nick!

He comes out from hiding and confronts me, like I know what is going on, yeah right!

"What's your nonno doing hitting on my nonna?" I ask and cross my arms against my chest.

We get into it a bit and then realise neither of us have a clue as to what is going on. I guess we can find out more by going into the church and doing some more spying, so I head over to the door.

"It's locked!" I stand there frustrated, and then Nick says something very weird.

"Probably gone to talk to the priest about the collection money."

What the hell is he talking about? Collection money? I've got enough to worry about a photo and the nonni kissing, so we decide to head inside the main door of the church and Nick starts giving me a tour. He shows me the dead saint body-thing with the gross, rotting teeth. It looks like something out of a zombie apocalypse. He is acting all weird, like he is the church tour-guide, and he should be so proud of that, not!

Finally, he rambles on about this collection money. And what a gobsmacking story that is. I find out there's a box with both our grandparents' names on it, and they send money for orphans to the church. Been sending money for years, apparently! For orphans, or kids whose parents aren't around. It's all a bit weird. Why would these two people who live in different states of Australia have teamed up to send money to a church on the other side of the world?

I'm not sure whether this is a bigger secret than the photo, or if they are equally potent. We now have a photo and a collection box, and our grandparents are involved with both items. Weird.

"Our grandparents are keeping a huge secret from us," I call Nick over to the altar where the lighting is a little better. "And I have something to prove it."

"What?" he asks.

I pull the photo from my back pocket and hold it right under his nose. At first, his face is a bit 'whatever', and he's not so interested, like I am showing him a photo of my boyfriend.

"Take a closer look."

His face changes from dumb to amazed shock.

"It's your nonno and my nonna!"

Snap! I think the photo is better than the collection box any day. Although now we had to work out how to link the two secrets together.

What does it all mean?

We sit on the altar steps and discuss in whispers what we know so far. There is something to do with a bambino and the church, and that they were together as teens, hooked up even.

"Maybe they had a baby together?" Nick suggests.

"Gross!" I squirm, imagining Nonna being pregnant at my age and having a baby. What would I do if that were me? If it's true, I wonder what choices Nonna would have had?

"Maybe they didn't want it, or couldn't,' says Nick. 'You know they were pretty young."

Then if they did have a baby together, is he or she still alive and more importantly who is it and where are they? We try a process of elimination and work out whether it could be one of our parents or an auntie or uncle.

"Maybe the baby died?" I suggest. "And the church helped them through their grief; that could explain the collection box."

"No, 'cause the box doesn't say for children who have died," Nick explains the inscription on the box again to me.

"So, if the kid didn't die, maybe the church helped them with it." I add, "You know, that's what used to happen in the dinosaur age." Why were we sitting there coming up with a thousand different scenarios? I throw my arms in the air like a true Italian. "I'm going to confront them right now!"

I jump up. Nick pulls me back down, calms me, and explains that it's best that we don't make a scene here, not in the church.

Finally, there was silence. We were a bit shocked, or depressed, I don't know.

Then Nick just looks at me. Really stares, really.

"What are you staring at?" I shift about on my bum.

"I'm not staring, I'm thinking!" he snaps and then changes his focus and looks at the marble floor. His mood changes, he's pissed off, but I don't think with me, I think with his nonno. I don't blame him, I'm pissed off with Nonna, but no use being pissed. Do something about it!

"I saw you in the bar," he says slowly and a little sternly. "You know, with Marco."

"And?" like I need his permission to go to the bar.

I change the subject back to why we are here, "Anyhow, stop thinking, and start investigating."

"Huh? You want *me* to find out what's going on?" he asks, dumbfounded.

"Well, duh! I'm not going to do all the work here," I say and head towards the door. "This is half your problem too!"

As I look back, I see the freak they call Pasqua-something mopping the marble floors.

I wonder how long he had been there.

Did he overhear us?

Even if he did, he can't understand English anyhow.

## CHAPTER THIRTEEN ~ Nicola

Morning stabs through the shutters, and I lie in the trundle bed watching the mote-filled rays as they strobe gently.

Canon fire woke me at five a.m. as usual. It's tradition here apparently. Every morning in the week leading up to the *Festa*, five sharp canon rounds are fired from the plateau just under the terrace outside the Chiesa Madre.

I've never seen mornings like they have them here. If I'd paid more attention in English class during poetry recitals, I might have come up with a better word than pure. That's the only word I can think of to describe how crisp and clean the air is around Nonno's village first thing in the morning. Pure.

I can hear Nonno in the kitchen. He's been upset about something since the day after we went to the sacred mountain. I think my telling him about the collection box didn't help, though. I think he wanted to keep that act of charity a secret.

And that's what it is: an act of charity. For whatever reason, my Nonno and Signora Racana, Lia's grandmother, have been sending money back to their village to help underprivileged people—like Pasqualino. I figure it's like a Southern Italian version of UNICEF or World Vision, where you can sponsor a child.

Nonno's always been modest about his life, so I figure who am I to embarrass him by harping on the obvious. And Nonna Rocchina would have known about the donations, too. Nonno Nicola never did anything without Nonna knowing about it. Not even gambling at cards in the cafes around where Nonno lives. Somehow, Nonna Rocchina always managed to find out how much Nonno had won—or lost—at cards.

Nonno often says Australia gave him a helping hand when he really needed it. He told me once that if he hadn't been able

71

to escape Italy who knows what would have become of him. So, sending money back to help some struggling people back in his native village was probably Nonno's way of giving something back for all that he'd been blessed to receive.

I'm feeling pretty good about myself when I finally make my way to the kitchen. I'm hungry, but not really looking forward to the breakfast Mountain Nicola and his wife think I need: hard-boiled eggs, thin slices of prosciutto, and a thick chunk of pasta dura bread. All washed down with milk that is still warm from the udder of the cows they keep in the stable a few hundred metres away from the house.

I've offered to buy cereal, but they won't let me spend any of my money on food. Nonno says it will offend them if I refuse what they offer and go out and replace it with processed and sugar-laden cereal.

My plan of attack is simple. I sip the milk, nibble the ends of the bread, push the eggs around the plate, and, when the moment presents itself, I find somewhere to dump the lot, usually into the feeding pans of the three dogs that live permanently outside the front door: hunting dogs Mountain Nicola has trained to scent out rabbits and wild pigs. They don't let the food touch the sides of the pans; they guzzle it down so fast.

Then I go to one of the bars in the piazza and grab a custard-filled brioche, a Coke and a chocolate bar. Too easy.

Only, this morning Nonno is at the table, and he ushers me to my seat opposite him and directs me to start eating. He has the mirror-image breakfast in front of him.

Nonno doesn't say a word. He just glares at me and starts to eat, matching each of my mouthfuls.

Each time I try to say something, he raises a finger to his lips and goes on eating. We continue this until both plates are empty. Only then does Nonno Nicola say anything.

"You have never known deprivation," he says in a slow, measured tone, using his best Italian, the one he reserves for special occasions, like speaking at weddings, baptisms, birthdays... or funerals. "That's why you can toss good, honest food out to the dogs."

And that's all he says. Not one word more. Nonno just reaches over, pats my hands where they sit on the table either side of the empty plate and nods slowly. Then he gets to his feet and pushes himself away from the table.

***

Nonno takes a solitary walk every morning. He won't let Mountain Nicola accompany him. Usually, he's gone by the time I get out of bed, but, because he waited to make sure that this morning, I ate the breakfast put before me, I decide to follow him at a distance as he heads out the door.

"Nicola," Mountain Nicola calls after me and ambles to my side. We're standing in the cobbled street outside his small house, the path steep and narrow.

"Nicola," he repeats and presses the tips of his fingers together. "Is much better you don't ask too many questions. Forget the collection box." Then, in broken English he adds, "I was tell to your Nonno that not good idea brings here you, other of the family what is in Australia. But your Nonno stubborn man. Good man, but stubborn, and him not listen."

Now there's some news I didn't know, I think. Nonno Nicola is stubborn. Really?

"What's going on?" I ask. "Nonno's been acting very strange. Stranger than usual." I'm asking the question, but my eyes are on Nonno's back as I follow him as he makes his way up the incline toward the village piazza.

Mountain Nicola seems about ready to say something to me when his wife appears in the doorway. He turns when she approaches. She's smiling thinly, the way people do when they don't really smile.

"The *ufficino* called," she says without invitation to break into our conversation. "There's a full day's work for you if you hurry and get there now."

Mountain Nicola doesn't have a fulltime job. Very few of the adults in the village do. Like many others, he works piecemeal, whatever he can get, at whatever is available. Being good with mechanical things, Mountain often gets work with the local mechanic.

"Of course," he says over his shoulder, but his eyes don't leave me. "Tell Donato I'm on my way."

There's a kind of wistful longing in Mountain Nicola's eyes that holds my attention. I look from him to Nonno's slowly retreating figure over his shoulder.

"Nicola!" Adriana snaps, "You better get going." Then to me, "*Andiamo al mercato, io e te, si?*"

No, I think. I don't want to go the market, thanks anyway. I shake my head.

"I have to buy Pasqualino a present," Adriana presses. "He's sixty this week. There's going to be a bit of a party for him at the church after the procession. I thought you might help me…"

"Adriana, *basta*," Mountain Nicola says firmly. He nods at me, then toward Nonno. "Go," he says.

"Nicola!" Adriana's voice is suddenly harsher.

Mountain Nicola puts a finger to his lips to silence his wife, and then nods again up the incline. I nod back and take off after Nonno.

The narrow road winds left and right, snaking its way towards the piazza. I hang back just enough so that Nonno doesn't know I'm there and to be able to duck into a doorway whenever Nonno stops a few moments to chat with someone who recognises him.

I don't know how I know, but I know. Nonno skirts the piazza, makes a right turn by the barbershop and tucks into a side street that leads directly into the square outside the Chiesa Madre.

But if I'm somehow not surprised by where Nonno's going, I'm taken aback by who's waiting for him.

Lia's Nonna leans forward as Nonno Nicola approaches her, and they exchange a light kiss on both cheeks, and then stand whispering under a sprawling fig tree for several minutes before Don Francesco, the village priest, interrupts them.

As I watch from the cover of the laneway, Don Francesco shakes hands vigorously with both Nonno Nicola and Lia's nonna. Then he ushers them into the church through a small door adjacent to the huge main double brass doors.

I'm about to walk out into the open when I get another surprise. Lia appears suddenly from the opposite end of the square. She's on her own, and I can tell from the way she's squinting towards the door that she too has been spying on her nonna.

Before I think it through, I step out into her path and ask, "What's going on here?"

Lia is hot. I can see why Raff is off the planet with thinking about her. Not that I'm interested, not after the way she snubbed me on the plane and everything. No, not me, but I can see why guys like Raff would think she's worth making a play for.

Lia does something I've seen my mum do when she thinks Dad has said something she considers ridiculous; she folds her arms and puffs out her cheeks.

"What's your nonno doing hitting on my nonna?" she asks, stepping past me.

"Where you going?"

Lia doesn't answer but storms toward the door Nonno and her nonna had gone through, except that of course it's locked now. She stands there looking up at a balcony on the next level.

"Probably gone to talk to the priest about the collection money," I say because I can't see why else Nonno Nicola and Lia's nonna would be together. "Come on, I'll show you."

The interior of the Chiesa Madre is cool and tranquil. The marble floor is so clean it shimmers, and the pews polished to a brilliant sheen that reflects the light coming in through the leadlight windows.

I point towards the glass casing where the statue of the saint lies.

"That's Santo Benedetto," I tell Lia as though I'm a guide and she's a tourist. "If you look in his mouth there are teeth there. The saint's real teeth. They're a bit gross and stuff, but yours would be too after a few hundred years of not being brushed, eh." For some reason I feel slightly superior with this knowledge, both about the saint, and more significantly, the collection box.

I hate to admit it to myself, but I'm trying to impress Lia. No wonder I'm sounding like the village idiot.

But Lia ignores me. She looks round the church instead, then ushers me to the altar.

She says something about a secret and then pulls something from her pocket and thrusts it at me.

I give the photo a quick glance and shrug, "And?"

"Take a closer look. It's your nonno and my nonna!"

The photo is old and tattered round the edges.

"Look familiar?" Lia asks and holds the photo out to me again, though, when I reach for it, she doesn't hand it over but merely puts it closer to my face.

I stare at the photo, and I'm shocked. It's as though I'm looking at a photo of me! Well, me, but in olden day clothes, a plain white shirt and baggy grey pants.

Lia sits on the steps of the altar, so I do likewise.

The young guy in the photo looks just like me! He's smiling in the exact same way I smile in photos, like I'm hoping no one will notice I'm smiling because smiling makes me self-conscious.

"Is that your nonna?" I ask. Lia nods.

"Are you sure? I mean, this is a really old photo, like from…" I turn the photo over and there's a fading date on it, but I can just make it out: 1965.

"Why would my nonno have his arms around your nonna?" I ask, but don't wait for a reply. The answer is sort of obvious. Two young people. Two smiling young people. The guy has his arms wrapped around the young girl. Yeah, bingo...

"They weren't... you know... they didn't... have the hots for each other, did they?"

Lia looks at me as though the word stupid just got a whole new dictionary entry, with my face as the definition.

I pass the photo back to Lia and get to my feet. I'm feeling a bit light-headed.

"It's probably pretty innocent, right?" I try. "I mean, you know, they were young and..." But I can't stop thinking about the collection box with both their names on it. The collection box for children who have no family. The collection box that doesn't have my Nonna Rocchina's name on it!

I scramble to the back of the altar and pull the collection box out. I read the inscription to Lia.

*For the keeping of those children whose parents are unknown or unknowable.*

"Pasqualino told me that your nonna and my nonno are responsible for this. That they somehow got this going." I hold the collection box out at arm's length. "He told me that the church uses this box to collect money for people like him."

I almost drop the collection box when the next thought erupts in my mind.

"Why would my nonno and your nonna do that...unless...?" I think I'm going to be sick even as I speak. "Maybe they had a baby together."

Lia yelps something then pokes her tongue out and shakes her head like she's trying to get something really disgusting out of her mouth.

"Maybe they had a baby and…" I'm thinking hard now because this is all a bit too dramatic for me. "Nah… Nah… Maybe…"

"Maybe nothing," says Lia getting to her feet. "I know an ex-lover's standoff when I see it. And what's been going on between them is so icy cold… until that kiss outside before, that only two people who once really cared about each other could be that cold towards each other now. It makes perfect sense."

I look at Lia. She doesn't look like someone who's high on some foreign substance. She looks… Hot is what she looks.

"Maybe the baby died," she suggests suddenly, and then adds something about the church helping them out.

"And maybe the photo is just two mates having a laugh," I say because anything else is too awkward, maybe even a bit too bizarre. I mean, Nonno Nicola has a family back in Australia, and daughters, and a dead wife who really loved him, and…

And if what Lia is suggesting is true, then does that mean Lia and me might be related?

I think of Nonno giving Lia's Nonna a kiss after all the angst there seemed to be between them and none of it makes any sense at all to me.

Just then, another thought occurs to me. I try to push it from my mind, but I can't.

What if my nonno, my teenage nonno, and Lia's teenage nonna, did have a baby, but it didn't die? That would make sense of the collection box.

The inscription reads, *For the keeping of those children whose parents are unknown or unknowable.*

It doesn't mention dead children at all.

I swallow hard and get wobbly, so I rest up against the altar.

"You okay?" Lia asks but I hold a hand out to stop her getting to her feet. I need a sec to think this through.

Here I am, in Nonno's village. I'm here because he drew my name out of his hat. Not only that, but the draw was also rigged so mine would be the only possible name drawn.

And here's Lia. Dimple-girl. Pointy-end-of-the-plane Lia. She's in her nonna's village, too. Her nonna's village and my Nonno Nicola's village are one and the same village. Coincidence? No. They were both born here!

We're here at the same time.

The two nonni have avoided each other since we arrived. Normal? Not really. Do they know each other? It seems they do!

They have their names engraved on a church collection box for children whose parents are unknown or unknowable. Coincidence?

I don't think so.

I feel Lia's hand on my shoulder, and I look at her, the collection box still in my hand.

"It doesn't say anything here about dead children," I whisper, "Just children whose parents are not known, or can't be known."

The same thought seems to register with Lia the moment it does with me.

"Oh, my God," I say, "coming to the *Festa*. That's a cover up. This trip has nothing to do with coming to the one-hundred-and-fifty-year celebration for the Madonna." I gaze round the church and shake my head. "I bet my nonno and your nonna are here for the same reason. If they did have a child together, that child is probably still alive. That would explain this collection box, and why my nonno sends money…"

I stare now at Lia. She's still hot, but sort of startled hot because I think I'm freaking her out a bit.

"My nonno has been in Australia just over sixty years. He left here in 1967, and he's in his late seventies now," I continue. "That would mean any child he had before he left for Australia would be…"

And that's when I collapse on the steps and drop the collection box onto the marble floor. It clangs and bangs away from me.

"About sixty or so," I manage to get out. "The kid would be about sixty."

Lia wants to go find her nonna and my nonno right away. She figures they're hatching something with the village priest, and she's riled that her nonna hasn't been straight with her, but I convince her to take a deep breath and slow down.

I replace the collection box where it belongs and show Lia the statue of the Holy Mother my nonno had dedicated to his wife, my late Nonna Rocchina.

There's something else I know that I'm not sure Lia does yet, but I don't say anything because I still think that all this figuring on our part could be about nothing much at all. Or maybe I'm just wishing that.

I tell Lia to hold on to the photo, and that's when she tells me she's already mentioned it to her nonna.

"When I asked her who was the guy in the photo, she said it was nobody," Lia says. "Like, sure, I believed that."

Then Lia hits me with more news. She's been to see nonno, but he told her to scram, to tell her family something about not playing games with him.

"That was pretty smart!" I snap. "You get one photo, and you go ask my nonno about it. Why? It's just a photo."

Lia looks sheepish but replies curtly. "Well, it was just a photo then. I just wanted to get an answer, especially after my aunt and my nonna didn't even want to talk about it. Sure, it was just a photo. I guess I was curious about my nonna, as a teenager like me, you know. But now. Now, with that collection box, it's a whole lot more, right?"

"Yeah, it looks that way," I answer. "But we don't know for certain what's going on here, so let's see what's what, okay?"

Lia starts towards the entrance. I must walk quickly to catch up with her.

"The guys wanted me to ask you to come out with a group of

them tonight," I say quickly. "Raff, my cousin. You remember him from up on the mountain, right. Him and his mates are getting together at the amusements and sort of taking it from there. If you want to come along." I shrug. "Bring your cousin and some of her friends too, yeah. I mean they'll all know each other, right?"

Lia hesitates.

"Let's not say anything to the oldies just yet, okay?" I whisper because I hear footfalls at our back. I turn and there's Pasqualino, mop in hand. He waves when he sees us. I wave back, and a strange knot forms in my belly.

## CHAPTER FOURTEEN ~ Aurelia

I sneak back to Villa Racana before Nonna does. Well, I guess I'm much younger than she is so I'm obviously twice as fast. Zia Santina is nowhere to be seen.

Rosaria has gone to school. It might have had something to do with me lecturing her about how important school is. Here in the village, the youth don't have any ambitions, they just hang out, help out a bit and live off their parents, or in Rosaria's case her grandmother. I guess I see a little of myself in Rosaria without the helping out bit, and looking on the outside, don't like what I see, and who I am.

I'm not that ambitious and don't even have a part-time job, just leech off Mum and Dad. Haven't even thought about the future, like why, live for today is my creed, or was my creed. Being in this village and seeing how life is just the same boring day after day and how even the oldies just do the same thing day after day, I was concerned for Rosaria, and when I started talking to her about her future, careers and life, I realised I was really giving myself a good talking to. And I didn't just want to end up being an academic in accessorising fashion or an influencer. I want to do more with my brain; I am better than that. I used to be top of my class in primary, in high school, I just let it all go, too interested in looking good and looking good for guys. Anyhow, I guess I have had a small influence on Rosaria, a positive influence—and that feels good.

I hear the back door open, dive onto the couch and pretend like I have been lying about the whole time Nonna was away. I even close my eyes and go limp, like I've fallen asleep. Nonna tries to sneak past me, doesn't want to wake me up. I practice my acting skills.

"Huh?" I murmur, "Nonna?"

"Sleep," she whispers and keeps going.

"Nonna," I sit up, "where did you go? I was looking for you"

"Nowheres." She stops at the doorway to the corridor.

"What do you mean nowhere?" I swing my feet onto the floor. "You must've gone somewhere."

She looks uncomfortable, uncomfortable lying I'm guessing. But then technically she's not lying yet as she didn't give me a Pinocchio about where she was, she just said nowhere, and nowhere could be the church with Mr. Alberti and the priest.

"You rest." She is about to move away.

"Nonna, come and sit down," I pat the couch next to me. She mumbles about being busy and is about to leave when I get the courage to just ask straight out.

"Nonna, why do you and Mr. Alberti have a collection box at the church?"

"*Cosa?*" her eyes widen and she screeches at me.

"You know, money you have been sending to the church," I pause, "with Nick's nonno."

She sways over to the couch and plonks down, looks like she is going to faint. But I don't fall for the dramatics that Italians are good at, I'm good at them myself and can see straight through it. She wants to change the subject by feigning illness.

"Is nutink," she says. "You big sticky-bicky, what you doing at the church?"

"Nick found the box, not me, so I'm not a sticky beak," I reply, "And anyway, what were you doing at the church?"

"*Cosa?*" She likes that word; she answers the question again with a question.

"And with Signoro Alberti!" I raise my voice. I show her that I am serious, I want answers.

"Nutink!" she stands up, suddenly better, "I go to church to pray, is none of you busy-nissy."

83

Pray? Yeah right, pray that nobody saw you, pray that nobody finds out your secret, and pray that I don't tell anyone back home. I want to test her, to see if she would keep lying to me.

"Nonna." I know this one is a big one. I look her in the eyes and ask softly, "Did you and Mr Alberti have a baby?"

There! I'd come out with it. Nonna looks at me sadly, her eyes well up, her hands shake, and she opens her mouth to reply.

"Aurelia!" Zia Santina calls from her bedroom. Wha-? I thought my great-aunt wasn't home, but she's been in the house all along. Spying on me? What a weird person, or maybe she was having a nap. What I *do* know is that her timing is bad, for me anyhow, good timing for nonna.

"*Si*, Santina," Nonna composes herself and heads down the corridor.

Damn. I was about to get an answer, wonder what she was about to say. Another lie maybe. She didn't deny it. Well, I'm not sure she was going to accept it, but if she was going to deny it, she would have replied straight away, instantly in fact. And maybe Zia Santina's timing isn't a coincidence, maybe it's sabotage. Maybe she was listening, and even though we were speaking English, she could sense what it was about.

I had so many questions for Nonna, and I only got one out. I want to know what happened to the baby. Did they give it up for adoption? Or did the church truly have something to do with it? Is that why they send money? Maybe the church looked after the baby, but then it wouldn't be a baby anymore, it would be around... I turned the photo over like Nick had, the baby would be a grown adult now.

Who is it? Who in this village is it?

Damn!

Why are the families keeping this secret? They are making it bigger than the eruption of Vesuvius. Okay, so Nonna got pregnant, it's no big deal. But then I keep forgetting how all those years ago it would have been the biggest scandal ever. I know a pregnancy at my age can turn your life inside out and more, but I wonder what effect it would have had back then. I'm torn. What happened?

Maybe they were promised to others, matchmaking was a big deal back then.

I go to my room and start to plan what I'm going to wear that night to the *carnivale*. Marco will be there for sure, gotta look hot without looking skanky. I can't decide, there are clothes all over my room now. I can't concentrate and throw myself onto the bed, take out the photo and have another look. It's obvious they were in love, they looked happy, the way Nicola's arm draped over Nonna's shoulder was his way of saying "She's mine." And her other hand crossed her body and clasped his draped hand in a way a person who was so comfortable with the other would do. It didn't look like brand new love or a crush, it looked like a lifetime love. That's special.

I then wonder why, if they were so close and in love, were they so cold to one another in our presence, and then there they were greeting each other so fondly at the church.

They must have been forbidden to see one another, and then banished from their village, sent to the other end of the earth– separate and yet together, together in the same country and yet states and thousands of kilometres apart.

It's obvious that, when their relatives are around, they put on the act, like at the airport, in the min-van, at the Madonna, with Zia Santina, and, even when I was at Nicola's house, he put up a show in front of his relatives.

So, another question arises, did they know that the other was in Australia and did they keep in touch?

It's too much of a coincidence that they are in Castel Pulcinella Velato at the same time.

Did they plan to be in their village at the same time? And why?

I am guessing their families were at war even before she was pregnant; maybe they had hidden their romance for a while.

Maybe it *was* like a real Romeo and Juliet story. And why was there this disease within the Racana and Alberti families?

What had caused it?

Maybe that's another secret, bigger than the pregnancy.

## CHAPTER FIFTEEN ~ Nicola

Nonno Nicola doesn't get back to Mountain Nicola's place until just before lunch. By then, Adriana is back from the market stalls too, and she's laid out a spread that back home would have made little cousin Ricky salivate himself dry.

But I'm not interested in the food. It's Nonno I need to talk to.

For some reason, wherever Nonno is, Mountain or Adriana is close by. I don't know if it's me, or they won't seem to leave Nonno's side. It looks suspiciously like the latter.

I try another tactic.

"So, what did you buy Pasqualino for his birthday?" I ask Adriana suddenly. "You said you went out to buy him something. What did you manage to find?"

My Italian isn't perfect, but it's okay enough that I know she's understood what I'm asking.

I see everyone stiffen. They're like those casts from Pompeii of the people that got caught in the ash and lava from the volcano Vesuvius. I've seen photos of them in a postcard book Adriana has on the side table where they keep the TV remote. She and Mountain Nicola went to Naples for their honeymoon, apparently, and visiting the ruins of Pompeii was a highlight. Or so Adriana reckons.

"It's a tradition here," Mountain Nicola begins, less than convincingly. "Every year we have a raffle to see who buys gifts for the people who have no family of their own. This year...This year me and Adriana we get Pasqualino's name."

I grin at Nonno Nicola. He's standing by the front door staring at a spot on the far wall where garlic stalks hang to dry.

"Funny that," I say in English. "That's how Nonno picked me to come here. He drew my name from a hat. Like a raffle. Raffles must be the go for people from these parts, then."

Adriana nods and gives me a thin grin. I grin back forcefully.

"So, what did you buy?" I press.

I look at Nonno, but he's already moved to the kitchen table and sat down heavily.

There's a long silence before Adriana wrings her hands and announces, "Your Nonno was very kind. He put in some money too, so... so Giovanni and me... the three of us with your Nonno, we can get Pasqualino a gold crucifix... it's beautiful."

Adriana fusses at a drawer and pulls out a square jeweller's box. She opens it without a word and shows me the contents.

"Adriana and me were going to buy Pasqualino a jumper," Mountain says with a quaver in his rich Italian voice. "But you Nonno. He is very generous."

I touch the small crucifix lightly. "It's a nice gift. For a man without a family. But I thought that's what that collection box in the church was for. Looking after people without families. Kids without parents. Pasqualino must be special."

Adriana snaps the box shut and returns it to the drawer, then motions for everyone to sit and we take our places.

"Where'd you get to, Nonno?" I ask as nonchalantly as I can.

"I was walk round. You know, see some my friend in the piazza. We talk, catch up." Nonno wipes his lips with the handkerchief he keeps pressed into the top pocket of his waistcoat.

We eat in silence. I can feel the others looking at me. I eat ravenously, as though this is the greatest meal of all times, and I'm the hungriest I've ever been. And just when Nonno is about to get up and move to the sofa by the window for his siesta I ask, "Why did Lia, Aurelia's granddaughter come here?"

It happens again. Nonno has a turn, right there in Adriana's kitchen. He shakes his head, wobbles his arms and then his forehead hits the table with a thud that makes me jump.

"Nonno!" I yelp and dive across the table.

Mountain is there first, his arms scooping Nonno up and sitting him back in his chair, Adriana at his side a moment later with a glass of water, most of which she pours over his face.

"Nonno!"

Mum is going to so kill me when she finds out I've given Nonno a heart attack. After the man's taken me to the other side of the world on what should be the trip of a lifetime for a kid from Fitzroy, Melbourne, Victoria, Australia, I kill him!

But Nonno's not dead. He's making low guttural sounds. The kind of sounds kids make when a teacher announces a surprise test. Or the kind grandparents make when they're totally shattered by the lack of respect shown to them by their ungrateful grandson.

"Nicola, please, you go find something to do, okay," Mountain Nicola advises me. "You Nonno needs to rest. You ask too many questions." Then I hear him whisper to Nonno in Italian, "I told you it was a bad idea for you to come with someone. Better you came alone."

I feel a pull at my elbow. It's Adriana. "No make the trouble, Nicola, please," she says in the English she's picked up from American TV. "You go to the piazza. The amusements will be opening soon. Let your nonno rest," she adds in Italian.

I want to demand some answers. I want to ask about the collection box. I want to ask about the photo Lia showed me. I want to know why Nonno was so rude to Lia.

I walk out instead and find myself taking the back streets to Villa Racana.

As I walk something makes itself apparent to me. The last time Nonno had a turn we were on the sacred mountain, and he had just introduced me to Pasqualino.

And just now, it was talk about Pasqualino's upcoming birthday that set him off again.

By the time I get to the wrought iron gates of the villa, I've worked up the courage to go to the front door and ask to talk to Signora Racana. If Nonno is having a turn whenever Pasqualino is mentioned, then I figure my calculations are more than mere coincidence, and it's time someone told me—and Lia—the truth about why we're here.

I'm about to knock on the door when I remember something else about my nonno's first turn. When he collapsed on the mountain after introducing me to Pasqualino, Lia's nonna approached and asked after Nonno, and she made what at the time seemed a strange comment, "The church isn't such a bad thing, Nicola."

I remember because at the time I thought it was such a random comment to be directing at me—or Nonno.

But if the comment had been directed only at Nonno, then it wasn't so random anymore.

*The church isn't such a bad thing, Nicola.*

The collection box with both their names on it.

The photo of a youthful Nonno Nicola, and an equally youthful Aurelia.

The two of them meeting with the priest.

And the special birthday.

"Nicola!"

I startle. Rosaria, Lia's cousin is at the door. She steps out onto the landing and smiles at me.

"Lia is no here," she says before I can ask. "She go with her nonna to the market stalls. They go buy something for Pasqualino. Is hims bersday same day of the *Festa*."

I look at Rosaria and nod. "Your family got his name from the raffle too?" I say with as much sarcasm as I can generate, and she gives me the kind of look I'm accustomed to getting from girls, the "So, did you think of that line all by yourself, loser?"

I'm running before Rosaria can ask me to explain and almost run into the barking dog on the way out. It must have been sleeping when I'd entered and only now was making up for lost time by snapping at my heels.

"*Basta!*" I yell at it and the dog stops stone cold still and merely whimpers at my back. *Stupid dog*, I think and keep running.

I don't find Lia, but Raff and his mates find me. They've all taken the afternoon off to get as much out of the *Festa* as they can. By nightfall, every road leading into and out of Castel Pulcinella Velato will be clogged with cars, trucks, buses, and even wagons pulled by stubborn, flea-bitten mangy mules and scrawny horses, they tell me with too much delight.

"You see wot party we have here," Raff slaps me on the back. "Not just in Australia do you have the big party, Nicola."

I really don't want to get caught up with this group just now, but I have no choice. I decide I'll catch up to Lia later. This place is only so big, and that's not big at all.

Adriana is right—the amusement rides start up by mid-afternoon. The travelling carnival has set up at the bottom of the main road leading from the village to the sacred mountain, in a vacant sprawl of land bordered by chestnut trees and the odd orchard.

Someone in the group gets it into their head that, since I'm from Australia and have travelled a long way by plane, I must have a heap of money, and so I can foot the first shout for the entire group.

It's easier not to argue, so I buy a roll of tickets, and we hit the rides. This is no Luna Park, but they have dodgem cars, a small Ferris wheel, and something that resembles a giant octopus whose mechanical arms toss riders high into the scorching Italian sun and then drive them almost into the ground again.

Marco, the suntanned, muscular Agip worker, sidles up to me as we line up to ride the miniature roller coaster and elbows me gently in the ribs.

"That girl, she coming to the party?" he asks out the side of his mouth.

"Maybe," I say shortly because I don't have a good vibe about this guy. He's all sleaze and toothy false charm. Worse than Raff. Back home we'd call him a tosser. Tosser!

"Is dance party," he tells me as we step forward and take our seats. Marco sits beside me in the leading car. Raff sits in the car behind.

"Australian girls, they very nice, yes?" Marco asks.

I shrug. He laughs a fierce laugh that shows all his back teeth. I don't like him much at all. I make a note to keep an eye on him around Lia.

Not that I'm a knight in shining armour or anything, more like an interested third party. But hopefully not just the third wheel.

It's nightfall by the time the boys have had their fill of the rides. I'm about to take my leave and head back to check on Nonno Nicola when Raff takes me aside and tells me there's no need, that it's the done thing here for the young people to party late on the Friday and Saturday leading to Sunday's procession. No one is going to come looking for me, he assures me, and Nonno is fine.

"You can come with me," Raff suggests.

"Where to?"

Raff is silent a moment. "Pasqualino. He comes with us every *Festa*. Don Francesco lets him come with us, but just for the Friday night. We have him back not very late."

Raff breaks off from the main pack and I walk with him.

"*Perche*? Why?" I ask.

"Why? Why what?"

"Why does Pasqualino come with you? He's a middle-aged man!"

Raff narrows his eyes and swallows. He pulls at the neck of his tee shirt. "Tradition," he blurts.

I smile, and then I laugh. "Like, what, you pulled his name out of a hat and now you have to entertain him every *Festa*, is that it?" I can hardly hide my sarcasm.

The group behind us snigger at something then Marco waves them towards the dodgem cars, with a call to Raff to make sure I bring the "Australian girl."

We walk in silence towards the Chiesa Madre, through narrow stall-lined streets, amongst the aroma of sausages sizzling over open grill plates and the cries of encouragement from the vendors eager to sell their wares; everything from plaster images of the Madonna and Child to plastic replicas of the Chiesa Madre.

When we reach the church, Pasqualino is already waiting for us. I hardly recognise him by the clothes he's wearing. Gone are the drab browns of his work tunic, replaced by jeans and a hoodie with a Ferrari logo across the front. He steps forward as Raff and I approach.

"Please, look after him, *ti raccomando.*" The voice catches me by surprise. It comes from the shadows, and I don't see Don Francesco until he steps out of the alcove, hands wedged together tightly.

"*Si, senz'altro,*" Raff replies quickly. Of course.

Don Francesco smiles and nods in my direction. "Nicola Alberti," he says matter-of-factly. "You look just like your Nonno."

I nod a stiff reply and shake the priest's hand when he offers it to me.

"Pasqualino," Don Francesco adds. "I need you to be alert for the services tomorrow and the following day." He turns to Raff and pointing a finger dramatically says, "I do this because Don Donato started it, but I will put an end to it if Pasqualino is made a fool of. You know I mean what I say, Raffaele."

Raff nods and, with the sacristan between us, we walk back the way we came, Pasqualino grinning at every stall, brushing his fingers along every piece of bunting, until he finally drops an arm over my shoulder and says, "Nicola Alberti is a good man. He and Signora Racana are good to Pasqualino."

I'm not sure why, but right at that moment I want to cry. I don't, though. Instead, I buy Pasqualino a thick pork sausage, shout another for Raff and take a huge bite out of my own.

I look like Nonno Nicola, but Pasqualino is his. I know this with a kind of deep belly tightness that makes me want to throw up at the same instant that I want to hug this man who is my uncle. I do neither, choosing instead to play along with Raff, with Mountain Nicola, with Adriana, and with Nonno Nicola too because for years this open secret has managed to survive and prosper without my interference.

I wonder though how much Mum, Zia Angela and Zio Nick know.

And I wonder how much Nonna Rocchina knew.

Those last thoughts make me sad. Sadder than I've felt since Nonna died. It's like suddenly this whole new world has been made known to me, and I'm sort of at the centre of it without really wanting to be.

And Lia, what is she to me? I think as we rejoin the boys who surprisingly come straight over and shake hands with Pasqualino, two of them taking him aside and urging him to ride the Ferris wheel with them.

"Look," says Raff at my left ear. "Lia she is bring. Rosaria with her. And some more girls."

I look down the main road, and sure enough, weaving their way slowly through the crowd is Lia, her cousins and friends with her. I raise a hand in greeting, and notice that Lia isn't smiling.

It doesn't take me long to find out why she isn't. Seems she and her nonna had a bit of a confrontation that afternoon.

Funny that. Must be something in the air. I don't tell Lia that of course. I take Lia aside before Marco finishes his stint on the mechanical octopus and tell her what happened with Nonno Nicola and me. I tell her what I suspect. I tell her it's the only logical answer. I put all the known facts before her, and she nods at everything I say.

"It just all makes sense," I say eagerly. I point to where Pasqualino is riding the Ferris wheel. "Look at him closely. Like you told me to do with that photo and tell me you can't see my nonno in him. I didn't notice it before. I mean, why would I? But after all I've thought about, and all the coincidences, including both of us being here, this year, not last, not next… but this year when Pasqualino turns sixty, it's just too much, don't you think?"

Lia Racana blinks slowly. Her eyes are misty, but she's not crying. There's a flush of red on her cheeks, but she's not wearing heavy makeup. She looks divine. I swallow and have to look away.

"I'm going to confront Nonno Nicola, though," I announce. "I need to hear it from him. I need to know that what I suspect, what we both suspect, is true. And I want to know why he just abandoned Pasqualino like that. It's not right."

And that's when Lia touches me gently on the arm and puts a finger to her lips.

"They were kids," she says softly. "My nonna, your nonno. They were like us, teenagers. But…" Lia hesitates. Rosaria steps in to ask if she wants to ride the dodgem cars and Lia shakes her head. When Rosaria moves off, she continues. "I talked to Nonna. I wanted to know about the photograph, and the collection box, and why she and your nonno met outside the church."

"And?"

But no sooner do I get the question out, than Marco ambles over, smiles broadly and threads an arm through Lia's.

"Come, *signorina*, I was show to you some good Italian hospital," he says smugly.

I think he means hospitality, but I don't correct him. Lia mouths the word "later" and lets herself be led toward a bank of garishly glowing sideshow tents.

## CHAPTER SIXTEEN ~ Aurelia

I just rested yesterday, being so exhausted from Friday's adventures of following Nonna, then confronting her before the day ended with meeting everyone at the *carnivale*. Well, not everyone… well, yes, meeting them but not hanging out with them 'cause Marco dragged me away—and, yum, we kissed! Aagh!

I have now officially kissed an Italian guy, a real one from Italy, not just one like me in Brisbane who has Italian grandparents but is born in Australia, but a real live Italian guy, and a super hot one. He sprung the kiss on me; he must have planned it somewhere between leaving Nick, who didn't look that happy, and the Ferris wheel. We were on the Ferris wheel, and you know how they stop sometimes mid-cycle. Well, he'd had his arm around me the whole time, then he just pulls me closer to him and gives it to me, the kiss, that is. It was pretty hot and heavy, I couldn't really pull away, where I was going to go? I was stuck in the bucket. Not that I wanted to pull away. We only stopped kissing because the wheel cranked up again and started moving. And who was waiting for me down below but Nick, Cousin Raff, and Pasqualino, who looked real strange, hanging out with people not of his own age. My stomach felt uneasy, but at the same time there was warmth in my chest. He grew up without his parents and why weren't they there for him? Strange, I have gone from thinking Pasqualino's a freak to feeling sorry for him. Especially if Nick is right, and that he is Nonna's son. I want to throw up.

"Lia," Rosaria waved as she headed over. Good timing, I didn't want to be there anymore, seeing Pasqualino spoiled the evening. Not that it was his fault, just, you know, the truth can be a cruel blow.

All this time we have wanted to know and now that we think

we know, I don't want to know!

So, I asked Rosaria to take me home. After she managed to drag me from Marco's arms, he had this hungry look in his eyes. It's probably a good thing I went home.

Rosaria brought me a cup of camomile, "*Domenica e la procession!*" she excitedly told me about the procession of the Madonna. I sipped my tea, and we talked about what happens at the procession and the church. It's the big day that the whole village has been waiting for all year. They cart a huge replica statue of their beloved Madonna all through town, from the piazza up to the Chiesa Madre, and then they have a huge party.

"*E anche il compleanno di Pasqualino, il sacristan,*" Rosaria said, pleased, "*fa sessanta.*"

Pasqualino is turning sixty? Sixty. I would not normally have cared. Hang on—maybe I do care. He was also a child without parents. Maybe Nick is one hundred percent right. Oh, I don't want to think about it, don't want to think that maybe Pasqualino is the baby that we are looking for.

I went to sleep and dreamed of people carrying me through town like the Madonna statue 'cause I was so tired. But they didn't carry me to the church; they took me to the cemetery, I was really upset in the dream, because everyone thought I was dead, but I was alive! Hate those kinds of dreams; you know, the ones that make you feel weird all day.

I wake to a beautiful Sunday morning where the household is abuzz with preparing for the procession. Everyone dresses in their best clothes and meets in the piazza, village central, just after lunch. They aren't even having their traditional afternoon nap today. Sacrificing it for the Madonna! The procession begins. Loud sirens, music bellowing not only from handheld stereos but also musicians who walk alongside the statue. Four men hold the statue on their shoulders; it's slightly morbid, like they are holding a casket at a funeral. Everyone walks very slowly. The priest mumbles stuff in Latin as he leads the way, and he is accompanied by that piano accordion guy, Pasqualino, and about half a dozen ladies who are chanting after the priest. It's all a bit odd but there seems to be a joyous atmosphere, can't describe it, festive, everybody is happy, so hey, I'm going along with it.

We head up the hill to the Chiesa Madre and along the way I catch sight of Nick, his creepy cousin and their friends. They weave in and out of the crowds, cheer and dance. Maybe they're drunk 'cause it looks strange for guys my age to act this way, guys back home have to be totalled to even think about joining a religious procession.

I catch sight of Marco; he's so gorgeous that I also catch my breath. He spots me, comes over, and joins me in the walk up the hill.

"You berry beautiful," he smiles.

Berry? Am I a strawberry, blueberry or raspberry? Who cares, how cute is it? He learned some English words; I'm sure courtesy of Nick, who I notice is watching from the side.

"So are you," I mutter shyly. "You're hot…"

"*Cosa?*" he asks, he can't understand English.

Marco flags Nick over and asks him to translate, which is funny 'cause I can speak better Italian than Nick!

"What did you say to him?"

"Um, that he is hot!" I laugh.

"*Lei pensa…*" Nick starts.

"No!" I grab Nick's arm, "don't tell him!" With that, I looked at Marco—"*Che bella giornata*"—and talk about the weather. He then gets that I speak fluent Italian, and his gorgeous smile becomes even more gorgeous.

"You can go now, Nick," I make eye and eyebrow movements for Nick to move on, he is a third wheel, and I want to continue on from what Marco and I were up to on Friday night.

Marco grabs my hand and holds it as we walk. I turn to see Nonna about twenty steps behind me with a dark look on her face and she does that thing with her lips like a cat's bum. I ignore her, no guilty Italian stuff now thanks, as I have the hottest guy in the village, maybe the whole country, holding my hand.

The procession finally makes it to the top, everything stops, the music, the people and the priest. It took a couple of hours to get there, everyone gathers their breath, and the priest opens the main church doors and lets everyone through. I step forward, but Marco pulls me to the side. He waits for everyone to enter the church and walks me around to the side where there is a concrete seat. Good thinking. I'd rather be with him on a love seat than in some old church with a thousand people and their garlic and anchovy breath.

Marco pulls me down onto the seat, and we lock lips. He is a pretty good kisser, so I don't pull myself away at first. He is getting pretty hot and heavy, and so I unlock myself to have a breather. Oh, boy, they move fast here in Italy. I thought they pinch your bum first, and then gradually move up and that it takes years to court a girl.

His eyes are intense. Marco stands up, takes me by the hand and leads me behind the church where it's more secluded. Very secluded. Nobody around 'cause they are all in church. I don't understand why we had to move—the love seat is fine with me. Hmm, I don't know whether I want to be there, I have this yucky feeling in my stomach. I mean kissing is one thing, but what does he want to do around here? Back home, I won't even go to second base until I know the guy a bit longer than this.

And then it's not long before I find out why he wants to be behind the church. He starts to kiss me again, but with a hunger. It's not until his hand starts to go up my shirt that I push him away with a loud, "*No!*" He just laughs, grabs and pins me against the church wall, his octopus hands continuing up and down my body, in and out of my top and jeans.

My cries are deafened by the church patrons' voices as they sing their psalm. How did I get myself into this? Where is Nick when I need him? This isn't fun anymore. I have to fight my way through this. His mechanic's arms are too strong for me. My heart is beating so fast I think I am about to have a heart attack. He throws me to the ground, straddles me and holds my arms down.

"*Fermati!*" a voice booms from behind. Marco looks up at the person and back down at me. I can't see who it is. Marco stands up, dusts himself down, runs his hands through his hair and walks off. I am lying there with my shirt ripped apart for the whole village to see.

"Are you okay?" Nick rushes in and helps me stand up.

"Yeah, I'm fine," I button whatever remaining buttons there are on my shirt. "Thanks."

"Don't thank me," Nick says, "I just got here."

He points. There behind me is Pasqualino.

"*Signorina,*" he shyly bows his head, "*la polizia?*"

"*Grazie,*" I walk over to him, take his hands in mine and thank him. And, yes, I am definitely going to report the assault to the police.

Pasqualino starts to walk away. I watch him and remember what Nick told me at the *carnivale*. But he's the one who saved me. He's a hero, not a freak.

Then I cry. I can't stop myself, I am in shock. I bawl like a little kid. I have been assaulted—I have the right to cry. Nick comforts me and explains that apparently Pasqualino was one side of the wall and could hear my calls for help from the other side, so came out to investigate. When Nick saw Pasqualino sneaking out, he decided to follow him. The priest put mass on hold to find out where Pasqualino was.

Word of what happened must have spread because everyone piles back out of the church. Nonna runs over and throws her arms about. Some of the villagers stand around in silence as Nonna curses an absent Marco, the village and Italy.

"Calm down, Nonna," I sniffle. "Thanks to Pasqualino, I'm all right."

Nonna is suddenly silent and is joined by Nick's nonno. They both stand there, look at Pasqualino, then at each other, then at Nick and me. They walk over to Pasqualino, thank him, and then Nonna starts crying too.

The priest heads over to the three of them and talks in a low voice. He takes Pasqualino's hand and places it in Nonna's, then takes Nick's nonno's hand and places it on top of theirs.

"*Buon Compleanno, Pasqualino,*" the priest announces. There is a silence, followed by shouts, laughter and crying. The villagers congratulate him.

"*Auguri, auguri.*" The villagers obviously know something we don't, and the priest has just blessed or done something to our grandparents and Pasqualino.

Pasqualino hugs Nonna and Nick's nonno. He looks like a little boy who's got lost in a crowd and just now found his parents.

I look at Nick, his eyes water. I have that weird feeling in my stomach. Nick turns to look at me, and then we both look at our grandparents and Pasqualino.

There is a real familiarity about the sacristan.

His nose.

Nicola Alberti's nose.

His eyes.

Nonna's eyes.

Now I know what the villagers know, what the priest knows, what everyone knows.

There is one other person who didn't know the secret.

Pasqualino.

Pasqualino is the baby.

Pasqualino is *their* baby.

## CHAPTER SEVENTEEN ~ Nicola

I chose not to hang around too much longer on Friday night. What with Pasqualino right there all the time, Raff trying to hook me up with every girl of marrying age he could find, and Lia off with "Marco the pretty boy", I made some lame excuse about not feeling well and went back to Mountain Nicola's house.

I didn't have the heart to confront Nonno.

No, that's a lie. I just didn't have the guts to confront him. Maybe it was because I knew there was nothing to be gained by getting Nonno all worked up about what I knew about him and Lia's nonna. Maybe it was because seeing Pasqualino close up like that, when he was just one of the boys, laughing along with Raff on the rides, eating popcorn and guzzling Coke like the rest of us. I guess it made me sad all over again.

Sad to think that maybe something bad, really awful, must have happened between Nonno and Lia's Nonna for them to have a baby together and then leave him behind like they did.

It had to be something bad because I didn't want to think of my Nonno abandoning his own kid.

I'm trying to forget all this, and the meal we had in deep silence last night when Nonno knocks on my door and peeps his frazzled head in.

"I come in, yes?" he says and shuffles in before I can answer.

"The cannonfire," he says softly, "she was wake me. I'm no use to it no more." Nonno sits on the end of my bed. He stares off into the distance and nods his head like he's thinking of something. It scares me so I try to make small talk.

"The cannonfire woke me too," I say, "But I'm thick so it didn't really register. I thought I'd farted loudly."

Nonno smiles, but it's a tired smile that droops quickly into a frown.

"Tomorrow is a special day," Nonno begins in his dialect. "The Madonna's one hundred and fifty celebration. Is a very special celebration. You see how many people come to the village, Nicola? Thousands of them, from so many places—even me and you, from Australia."

I'm not that thick that I can't see an opening when it's in front of me.

"And Lia and her nonna, too," I say, but the words almost catch in my throat, and they come out sort of muffled, like I've got a mouthful of two-day old bread.

There's a fork of daylight coming in through the slats of the wooden shutters. They cascade over Nonno's knobbled hands where he has them folded on his lap.

"When Don Francesco wrote to me, saying I should come here for Pasqualino's special birthday," my nonno whispers, "I knew I couldn't come back here alone, Nicola. I was just a few years older than you are now when I left. I was a young man, still a boy in so many ways."

"And a father," I toss in before I can stop myself.

Nonno startles for just a second. I think maybe he's having another turn but, no, he's crying softly, tears flowing down his brown paper bag face.

I reach out and touch Nonno's hand. He looks at me.

"I had a child, but I was not a father, Nicola," Nonno continues. "I was scared. Aurelia was scared. We were so young. She was from a family I had no right to have anything to do with." Nonno draws a breath.

I'm about to jump in with a comment about anything not related to what he's trying to tell me when he pushes on.

"Aurelia was promised in marriage to someone," Nonno announces, and I see him tremble a little. He wipes his nose with the back of his hand then tries to take mine again. Yeah, well, not good, but I have no choice, do I?

"The other family," Nonno says, louder now. "The other family was wealthy. Wealthier than Aurelia's family. They were a family who could afford to marry their son to a beautiful flower like Aurelia. My family, we were goat herders and peasants. We grew olive trees and sold cheese in the piazza. What could I offer Aurelia?"

"Love," I piped up. I don't know where that came from. Lia's influence maybe? Yeah, right, we've really spent a lot of time together.

I must have said the right word though because Nonno suddenly smiles and claps me firmly on both cheeks. "Love, Nicola. But in a little village like this one, with so few opportunities after the war, I had nothing to offer. Love was not enough."

There's a weight sitting in the pit of my stomach, and it has nothing to do with all the crappy food I ate on Friday night, or yesterday when I pigged out on the cannoli and tiramisu Raff's mum brought over for dessert after the family meal.

The weight shifts and stirs as I listen to Nonno talk. I'm thinking of him as a young man. I'm thinking of Lia's nonna as a pregnant teenager who's promised to the man who is not the father of the child she's carrying.

And I'm thinking suddenly of all the years Nonno has been separated from his son, Pasqualino.

"Is that why you send money," I say, "to the collection box, with your name and Lia's Nonna's name on it? The one Nonna Rocchina didn't know about?"

"You're wrong, Nicola," Nonno says and narrows his eyes. "Your Nonna Rocchina was an incredible woman. The collection box was her idea. She told me that even though I'd left my past behind, I could never leave someone who was my blood relation behind. Your nonna was the one who made me find Aurelia after so many years. She was the one who convinced us both that Pasqualino was not at fault for something that even we two, me and Aurelia, could not control. They were strange times back then, Nicola. People had strange ideas about having children out of wedlock. And yet there are so many of those children. So many..."

Nonno fell silent. He sniffled and wiped his nose and finally got to his feet.

"I'm very sorry I was bring you here, Nicola," he adds and shuffles to the window, throws the shutters open and lets in the brilliant Sunday morning light.

"I never should have bring you here," he continues, his back to me. "But you got my name, and I was think maybe was like me be young man again and..."

I don't let Nonno finish. I jump out of bed and give him a huge hug. The kind of hug I think Mum will give me when I get back to Melbourne and walk through customs into the arrivals hall at the airport. A hug that tells me so much more than most words ever could.

"Pasqualino is pretty lucky to have a dad like you, Nonno," I whisper into the top of his bald head.

We stay like that for a few minutes until we hear the first strains of music floating down from the piazza. The bands are tuning up, getting ready for the procession, and me and Nonno have to do likewise.

"I won't say anything to Mum, or anyone," I say finally. "It can be a secret still." Sure, a secret only my Nonno, Lia's Nonna, Lia, me, Raff, Rosaria, Mountain Nicola, Adriana, and most of the rest of the village know about!

Nonno looks at me and shakes his head. "No, Nicola," he whispers. "When we get back, I have to be honest with you mother, with her sister, her brother..." Nonno waves an arm about, and switches to Italian. "No more secrets, Nicola. If only for you Nonna Rocchina's sake. She wanted me to tell our children about their half-brother many years ago. She was a wise woman. I am a silly old man."

"No, you're not a silly old man, Nonno," I say, and I mean it. I draw a breath and ask the question I want the answer to—the one I know Lia wants answered, too. "Do you still care for Aurelia?"

I feel Nonno stiffen under my touch. His shoulders square then fall.

"I love your nonna," Nonno says softly. "Aurelia is the mother of my son. My other son. They are both from my past, a past I cannot change, Nicola."

"Would you change it—if you could?" I ask.

For a moment, Nonno is silent. I listen to him breathing, each breath deep noisy, as though it's an effort.

"It is not for me to change," he answers finally.

Nonno steps out of my embrace and heads for the door.

I'm rattled but not surprised by what he's said. He's still scared, my Nonno. I know because he and I are so similar. I can sense his fear. But it's not a dark fear, more the sort of fear you get when you dare yourself to do something you know you'll be so proud of yourself for doing after the event. Like asking the prettiest girl in the class to go to the movies with you when you know there are heaps of other guys she'd probably rather go with, but you just must take a shot.

"Thanks for rigging the raffle so that I got to come here with you, Nonno Nicola," I say, using his Christian name for the first time in a long time, and enjoying the sound of it. "I love you. We all do."

Nonno walks out without a further word, but not before he gives me a smile and a pat on the head.

It's good. It's all good. Or it will be. For now, I've promised Raff and the boys I'll catch up with them for the procession.

## CHAPTER EIGHTEEN ~ Aurelia

It feels different on the flight home to when Nonna and I flew over to Italy. I guess I am different. I know things—more things— about my heritage, my family, my nonna, myself. And when you know things, other things, you aren't so ignorant anymore. You come to understand life a bit more than you thought you did before; so much more that little things may not shock you. Perhaps big things don't shock you anymore, like Nonna's secret baby.

Nonna and Nick's nonno are going to visit each other when we get back home now that everything is out in the open and the animosity has dissolved. That'll be cool, 'cause then I can catch up with Nick again and add him to my list of a thousand and one cousins. He's a cool guy—I'll put him on my list of best male friends.

I did report Marco's assault to the local *polizia*. Not sure what's going to happen yet, but he may just get a warning, so at least that's something. I still feel a little shocked about it, like what would have happened next if Pasqualino hadn't barged in. I am so grateful for him coming to my rescue. And to think the "freak" is related to me, my family. Goes to show, don't judge a book, blah blah. He's a really nice guy, old, but nice.

Nonna and Nonno Alberti have been sending money back to the church for years to help support him. Nonna told me that Nicola had started it, and then they or the priest asked her to contribute as well. But what I think happened is that Nonna found out and insisted with typical Italian pride that she was going to match him dollar for dollar.

Pasqualino is happy with living and working at the church. This is all he knows. He was really cute when we said goodbye.

"I coming to Australia one day," he said slowly, and then looked over at Nick, who nodded. It was obvious that he had practised the sentence with Nick. That was even cuter—that Nick helped him. I smiled at Nick and noticed he was wearing the stylish runners I helped him shop for. Well, I mean, if you are in Italy, you have to buy a new pair of shoes!

The whole village came out to wave us all goodbye; the drive back to the Rome airport was very solemn. I was going to miss Italy, my newfound friend and cousin, Rosaria, the *passeggiatas*, even Pasqualino and most of all I was going to miss the essence of Castel Pulcinella Velato, what a mouthful! Even though I wasn't allowed near the castle, I still appreciated its beauty from my balcony.

I wonder if that was Nonna's bedroom and whether she used my balcony when she was a teenager, she would have been a real Juliet. Listen to me, "my balcony". I did feel a part of this village. Well, I guess this is where my roots are, where my ancestors gave birth and buried their dead. Nobody really knows who lived in the castle, and why it was abandoned. I guess it has its secrets too. Talking about secrets, I guess it's time to fess up to Nonna about mine, 'cause, like Mum said, I have to face up to it when I get home.

"Nonna," I lean closer to her seat, "I have a secret, too."

"*Si*, Aurelia," Nonna puts down her magazine to listen.

"Sara and I were expelled from school." With shame, I look down at my feet, "um, because...."

"Aurelia, you no need tell me," Nonna takes my hand, "I already know."

"You know?"

Huh? My nonna knew all this time and didn't say anything.

"*Si*," she looks into my eyes. "Dat's why I take you on this trip, for you to get away from everything and everyone."

I give Nonna a big hug and have a little cry. She then talks about what it felt like to keep such a big secret from her family, in particular her husband. Wow, that must've eaten her up inside.

"How hard it is, Aurelia, when da family no support you," Nonna says as she wipes a tear. She tells me about the beautiful night that baby Pasqualino was born, at the church, down in the grotto with the Madonna, with the help of a local nun.

"*Una mamma*, a mother never forgets the moment her child is born, Aurelia," Nonna says.

It all makes sense now, why she has this obsession with the church and the Madonna. Not only did it help bring new life, but it also sustained Pasqualino's.

"Nonna, why didn't you and Mr Alberti get married and keep the baby?" I ask softly. I don't want to upset her any further.

"The Alberti family were poor, not good enough for me," she pauses, "so my papa said."

"I was promised to another, very wealthy, but when they find out, they call me a *putana*, a woman of the street," she says sadly. "My mamma and papa then send me out of the village to Australia in shame. I not seen my parents since." She begins to cry.

"Nonna, I am sure your parents were proud of you," I had a tear in my eye. "They just did what they thought was right at the time."

How sad. Nicola's and Aurelia's was such a young love, doomed from the start.

A tragic love story.

Nonna and I then talk about whether she is going to tell the family back home, whether Dad should know he has an older stepbrother.

"*Si*, no more secrets," Nonna exclaims. "I want to live—I want to breathe. Secrets make you have a heavy heart, Aurelia, like the *castello*, the castle."

"What about the castle, Nonna?"

"Castel Pulcinello Velato means the *castello* that wears the mask to hide its secrets—" she looks down at the ground as she is thinking, "like the veil the bride she wears to hide her face."

"What secrets does the castle hide, Nonna?" I am enthralled about these veiled secrets of the castle.

"Nobody knows, Aurelia," Nonna looks at me with sadness. "I think that's why the *castello* is rundown. She has a heavy heart, she has given up, her secrets are buried there, never will they be let out." Then Nonna smiles. "I am taking off my mask. I will not be buried with my secrets. I am not like the *castello*."

You go, girl. I mean, Nonna!

## CHAPTER NINETEEN ~ Nicola

"**M**arco is in serious trouble.

The *carabinieri* took statements from me and Raff, and Pasqualino too. They wanted to know what we heard, and what we saw when Lia was found after she cried out for help outside the church.

I told them the truth. I was sitting with Nonno after having followed the procession through the village with Raff and some of the guys. Not Marco though. Marco must have been plotting his move on Lia because we hadn't seen him all morning. The first I saw of him was when I followed Pasqualino out of the church and saw the dirty slimeball taking off in a hurry as I helped Lia to her feet while Pasqualino kept reassuring her she was safe now.

At first, Lia thought it was me who yelled at Marco to stop. It wasn't until I pointed out Pasqualino standing there that she realised he'd been the one to rescue her. When Lia started to cry, I didn't really know what to do, but Pasqualino did. I put an arm around her and tried to comfort her, and Pasqualino comforted her, told her not to worry, that he knew who Marco was.

And then it seemed that everyone who'd been in the church was suddenly there with us, surrounding us, even Don Francesco.

Lia's nonna almost lost it. She spaced out when she realised what might have happened to her granddaughter, but Lia was remarkably calm about it all. She told her nonna that luckily Pasqualino had scared Marco off.

That was almost a week ago now. Lia and her nonna are back in Australia. They flew out three days ago, after making reports to the local police and identifying Marco.

Nonno and me are having lunch with Pasqualino today. Don Francesco's arranged it. Just the four of us, in the dining room at the presbytery. I'm looking forward to it. Nonno has spent a bit of time with Pasqualino these past few days. Lia's Nonna not so much as she's been wanting to get Lia home as soon as possible.

I went to see Lia, to say goodbye, but it was awkward. I mean, with her nonna and my nonno having a kid, like, does that make us related? The thought makes my head spin!

Lia was cool about it all. Lia is cool. Full stop. Pointy-end-of-the-plane cool. Designer label cool.

Really good-looking cool.

Lia gave me her Brisbane address. She said to visit if I ever get to Queensland. I told her I'd do that, visit her. She gave me her mobile number so I could let her know in advance.

When I reached out to shake her hand, Lia pulled me into a hug. I must have been so embarrassed that I patted her on the back like she'd just kicked a goal or something and then I hugged Nonna Aurelia too.

Even now, I blush at the thought.

"Sixty years is a long time, Nonno," I say as the two of us make our way slowly up the incline toward the Chiesa Madre. It's a warm day, not a cloud in the blue sky, the entire village still slumbering after the weeklong celebrations.

"Is a lifetime, Nicola," Nonno says softly.

"How do you feel?" I ask. "About everyone knowing Pasqualino was yours and Nonna Aurelia's? It's not like it was a complete secret here after all." I was wondering what would have become of Pasqualino if all that had happened between Nonno and Lia's Nonna had happened in Australia, in Melbourne or Brisbane.

Nonno doesn't hesitate. "Blessed," he says and pauses in his stride. He straightens up and looks back down the narrow street that leads to his nephew's house, back to his childhood home. "Our son was allowed to stay in his village. I was allowed to see him again, even after all those lost years. I am blessed, Nicola."

I smile. I'm looking forward to having lunch with Pasqualino. I want to know how he feels about finally meeting his parents after all those years.

I thread an arm through Nonno's, and we set off again. "Pasqualino's the only member of the family who can play an instrument," I say suddenly because it's the truth, and the truth sometimes is so very basic you don't see it until it's pointed out to you.

Nonno grins and leans his weight into me. I steady him, and we head for lunch and a long chat with the latest addition to the family.

# CHAPTER TWENTY ~ Aurelia

"**M**um!" I dump Nonna and the trolley and run to Mum's open arms. We hug like maybe Pasqualino and Nonna hugged, like we haven't seen each other in years. I missed my mum. I missed our talks, our sitting down together every afternoon to watch that stupid soapie and have our afternoon tea. I even missed our fights.

I didn't miss what I had to come home and face, my expulsion and its consequences. I would have to find a new school, new friends, a new reputation—but then I was a new person, so that might all be a good thing.

A fresh start.

Like Nonna. She is going to have a fresh start, a second chance at being a mum to Pasqualino.

"So, what's new?" Dad asks as he loads our luggage into the car. Nonna and I look at each and smile.

"There's heaps new, Dad," I answer for both of us.

"You can tell us all about your trip once you've had a rest. They're jet lagged." Mum, being a mum, is giving us a break.

I can't wait to sit around the table and help Nonna share her news. Dad is going to be shocked, but excited at the same time I am sure, to know he has more family. Then who knows, maybe Nonna sharing her secret allows others to share theirs, as I did.

In the car, I sink back into my seat and feel safe, I realise that everything is going to be okay, I have learned from my mistake, hell yeah, I got expelled but I can move on now. And after being in the village, I've realised that some things just aren't that important, that is, I can live without the Internet, my fave jeans, shopping, and a hair straightener. And I don't have to be with my friends 24/7, and maybe I can even live without Sara!

114

The most important thing I have learned is that family is precious, just like diamonds. Some may have their flaws, but they are tough, and their beauty is what makes you love them.

Oh, yeah, but the best lesson I learned is that there's no use trying to keep a secret 'cause it's always found out.

Even after so many years!